MADDOX

HAWKE'S RIDGE
BOOK ONE

LEXI BUCHANAN

HFCA Publishing House

Ireland

ISBN Amazon Paperback 6x9 - 978-1-918152-16-6

www.lexibuchanan.com

First Published 2025

Copyright © 2025 by Lexi Buchanan

All rights reserved.

Cover Image: © Wander Aguiar Photography

Cover Image Model: Zack Salaun

Proofreader: Lynne Garlick

Cover Design: Alison Higson

Chapter One

Maddox

As I await a group of tourists arriving for a five-day stay in Hawke's Ridge, I welcome the summer breeze drifting over the airport at Anchorage. Hawke's Ridge is not only the name of the town where I live with my dad and seven brothers, but also the name of the Lodge we built and opened five years ago. Yes, you heard that right. I'm one of eight brothers, and we all play a role in running the Lodge. My youngest brother, Colton, has only been a permanent fixture for the past three months. He was too young to leave before that and wanted to stay and be there for Mom, who lives in Sugar Briar, Tennessee.

We take turns visiting her so she's never alone for too long. I guess we all get our independent streak from our father. Mom is one tough cookie, though, hence why she is still in Sugar Briar and dad is here in Alaska. Looking at her, you'd never guess that she gave birth to all eight of us. It's not something I dwell on too much because that's just too much information, you know?

Hawke's Ridge is a popular tourist spot, and I'm proud of that. It's a beautiful place with a lot to offer. It's an all-season Lodge. During the winter, only a Beaver or Cessna planes with skis can reach us. That's why I take advantage of picking up tourists with the bus whenever I can. I don't miss the city much when I'm home on the Ridge, but I do enjoy visiting occasionally, for a change of scenery.

My hair ruffles in the breeze as I catch sight of the Cessna 208 Caravan approaching the runway. It's carrying eleven women here for a bachelorette party. I wince at the thought. My brothers, Ryland, Hunter, and Garrett are looking forward to the next five days, which makes me chuckle. I can already imagine the chaos that will ensue. Personally, I'd rather work on my motorcycle than spend time with a group of women who are only interested in gossiping and drinking wine. This isn't the first bachelorette party we've hosted, and it won't be the last. That's why Dad and Spencer installed a couple of hot tubs on the back deck for the ladies to relax in while the guys hang out by the fire pit. It's worked so far.

We get hunters and fishermen at certain times of the year,

as well as families looking for a break from city life. We're prepared for anything at this point. Our guests always leave happy and satisfied with their stay, especially those who get eaten out by my brothers.

Chapter Two

Sofie

As THE AIRPLANE GENTLY TOUCHES DOWN ON THE RUNWAY, I wonder how long I'll be able to keep smiling. I've always dreamed of visiting Alaska, but when my boyfriend mentioned it to his sister, she thought I wanted to have my bachelorette party here. I couldn't imagine anything worse than spending my bachelorette party in Alaska with women I don't know and don't want to know. I didn't want a party. It's not my idea of fun. My idea of an idyllic setting is a cup of coffee, a good book, and a blanket over my lap while sitting on a porch with a view of snow-capped mountains.

My best friend, Jamaica, should be here, but my future

sister-in-law didn't want to wait an extra week for her to return from a work trip. I had no idea that things were being booked until Richard told me that I was leaving in two days. I was furious and knew Samantha had done it deliberately.

The door of the small plane opens, and a nice breeze wraps around me. I wait until everyone else is off before moving into the doorway. I take a deep breath, step out onto the tarmac, and close my eyes, inhaling the fresh air. I'm in Alaska! Excitement runs through me, even as the stupid veil we all wear whacks me in the face, reminding me of the harsh reality—I'm getting married in a month.

"Are you okay?"

My eyes snap open at the sound of the masculine voice. Dark brown eyes stare into mine, and I forget where I am. I gaze at his handsome features—strong cheekbones and a short, dark beard covering his lips and jawline. He's a hot guy. He's tall, but everyone is tall compared to my five-foot-four frame. His long hair is tied back. I notice tattoos peeking out from under the sleeve of his shirt as my gaze moves downwards.

His deep voice rumbles through his chest as he repeats, "Are you okay?"

My eyes shoot upward, and I see his lips twitching with amusement while my face heats. I clear my throat. "I'm good." I offer my hand. "Sofie Ryan."

He grins. "Maddox Hawke."

Out of the corner of my eye, I see something pink—Samantha. She wobbles toward us in her high heels and takes

Maddox by the arm. "Tut-tut, Sofie. It's your bachelorette party. You need to let the single ladies talk to the delicious mountain men." She tries to pull Maddox away, but he clenches his jaw, probably biting back a curse or two, before untangling himself.

"If you all get on the bus, I'll load the luggage." He nods and walks toward the pilot, who is unloading the plane.

Samantha turns my way. "My brother won't be happy about you flirting with the first guy you see."

I open and shut my mouth, knowing better than to argue with her. I don't curse. Well, I didn't curse until I met her. She's acting like she's jealous of me being with her brother, which makes no sense. I have my own money, so I'm not after Richard's. I can cook. However, I don't like his family, which might become an issue. So far, I've accepted Richard pushing me to spend time with his sister, even though he knows I don't want to. Anything I want seems to have gone out the window. I'm not sure what I'm going to do about it.

Recently, I've been considering canceling the whole thing. The reality is that I don't love Richard. In fact, on one or two occasions, I'm sure I haven't even liked him.

"Are you not getting on the bus?" The pilot breaks into my sad thoughts.

"I guess so." I don't make a move.

"If you want some free advice, you need a new set of friends."

I glance up at him, and he winces. "I might be the pilot, but I hear everything."

"They're not my friends."

"You don't want to be here?"

"I've always wanted to visit Alaska, but I wish I was here alone." Sighing, I put one foot in front of the other and climb onto the bus. The only seats are toward the back, so I head in that direction. I leave two rows between them and me.

Maddox steps inside and quickly glances around. A frown appears on his face when he spots me alone at the back. He blinks, and the curiosity on his face disappears. Samantha and her friends bombard the guy with questions, but he only grunts in response. Eventually, he ignores them.

The bus finally falls silent.

I yank the stupid veil off my head and rub my scalp where the teeth dug in. I wince as I pull my hair free of the elastic holding it in a ponytail. I massage the back of my head and slowly turn my neck to get the kinks out. It's been a long, stressful day of traveling with this group.

As we leave Anchorage, I finally get to see some of the views I've dreamt about, and a small smile slips onto my face. Wide open spaces and snow-capped mountains in the distance. Along the highway, there are trees and green spaces. We travel over a huge body of water and pass through another large town before heading out into the wilderness again. This time, the highway is smaller, and there are tall trees along the road.

I struggle to keep my eyes open and surrender to the losing battle.

When I open my eyes again, Maddox's low, sexy voice says, "Wake up, babe."

He's crouched beside my seat, but I can't read his expression. He stands, but not quite reaching his full height because of the roof of the bus and holds out his hand. "Come on, Sleeping Beauty. Your friends are already inside the lodge."

I take his hand. "They're not my friends," I mutter, letting him tug me to my feet. I meet his gaze and see questions in his eyes. "I should join them." He grunts and, intertwining our fingers, leads me off the bus. Why I don't pull away from this stranger is a mystery.

It's nice having my hand held in his. The touch sets off little fireworks in my panties. But that's wrong, considering the engagement ring on my finger. A little voice in the back of my mind reminds me that Richard never holds my hand nor sets off fireworks in my hooha from just his touch. What the heck is wrong with me? I try to tug my hand free, but Maddox won't let go.

Three men stand close to the luggage at the side and stare our way. Maddox gives them the finger which I'm sure I wasn't supposed to witness. He then leads me up the three steps to the lodge's entryway. He hesitates at the double doors and, with what feels like reluctance, let's go of my hand. I search his face, hoping he'll explain what's going on, but he says nothing.

The door in front of us bursts open, knocking me backward. If it weren't for Maddox's quick reflexes, I would be on the ground. Instead, I have Maddox's arm around me while he

9

glares at Catherine, Richard's mother. "What are you doing loitering out here with that man?" She gives Maddox such a snotty stare that my hackles rise.

"Catherine," I snap, shocking her, and myself, "this is Maddox Hawke, one of the owners of the Lodge."

Her eyes widen. "I'm so sorry. I'm not usually so—"

I cut her off. "Maddox, thank you for seeing me to the door. I'd better get Catherine inside." I step away from the man, feeling bereft as I do so. I take Catherine by the arm and lead her inside.

The moment the door closes behind us, she turns on me, as I knew she would. "What do you think you are doing?" She hisses, digging her fingernails into my arm. I wince and try to pull my arm free, but I can't. "You're marrying my son, so you don't talk to other men. Otherwise, I will make sure my son knows that you're a floozy!" With one final, sharp dig of her fingernails into my flesh, she lets go and moves toward her daughter.

Tears spring to my eyes as I join the line to check-in while wishing I had a letter opener to stab the horrid woman with. That thought drags a wince out of me. I'm not a violent person. As I give her a sideways glance, I think I might end up one.

I'm not going to put up with this crap anymore. When I get back home, I'm going to give Richard his ring back. I was slowly coming to the conclusion that I needed to end things when the trip was dropped in my lap.

I sigh wondering how I got into this mess.

Chapter Three

Maddox

I turn away as Sofie enters the lodge and trudge back to the bus, where Garrett, Ryland, and Hunter are staring at me. "What?" I snap, irritated.

Ryland snickers. "You're asking what's wrong with us when you held hands with the girl and walked her to the door? What was that?"

I open my mouth to say that I was just being friendly, but that would be a lie. From the moment I saw her step out of the Cessna, I knew she was different. I couldn't stop looking at the woman who exuded an air of loneliness. I was compelled to touch her. I wanted to keep her, and that threw my entire world into chaos. "I don't know," I tell my three brothers, only to spot a fourth moving toward us with a frown on his face.

I root through the luggage and find the case I was looking for. I turn to watch my brother, Gabriel, approach, wondering who pissed in his coffee.

I'm eager to head inside and find Sofie Ryan, the woman whose sad eyes drew me in and whose scent lingers after our brief encounter. My visceral reaction to her is unexpected and new to me.

"What's going on with them?" Gabriel nods toward the main building. "They're not very friendly to each other." He shakes his head. "The girl Garrett texted me about was getting chewed out by an older woman."

"What the fuck!" I snap irritated at my brothers for gossiping, but I'm more furious that someone would hurt my woman. My woman, huh? For once, that doesn't scare the shit out of me. "Just to be sure, honey-colored hair?"

Gabriel stares my way. "Honey-colored?" His mouth twists into a grin. "Caught your attention, has she?"

"Was it her or not, Gabe? I'm not in the mood."

He rolls his eyes. "Yes, it was her. Garrett described her well. Has your shorts in a wad, huh?"

"Fuck!" Ignoring the snickers from my four brothers, I rush up the steps and inside. My eyes immediately lock onto Sofie at the reception desk. The woman from the airport talking a mile a minute to her. I frown wondering if Sofie is supposed to be sharing a room with barbie.

Oh, that is not happening!

I quickly make my way behind the reception desk and call Colton, my youngest brother, over to me. "Make sure you give Sofie Ryan a double room. I don't want her sharing with anyone."

He gives me a knowing look. "Um, okay."

I narrow my eyes. "I'm not sure what's going on, but she's the odd one out. I'd rather she has someplace to go for some peace."

"That's not good. I'll go take care of it now." I grab him by the back of his shirt. "Bro, what the fuck is your problem?" he hisses.

"Get me the keycard. I'm going to take her to the room. I'll cover the additional cost."

"You're acting fucking weird, but okay." Colton shakes his head. Back at the reception desk, he smiles and flirts with the uppity Barbie while handing her a keycard. Then he passes one to Sofie. I know he's explained that they're in different rooms when Barbie's face turns red with anger.

That's my cue!

Samantha spots me moving toward them first and perks up, while Sofie turns and offers me a small smile. "Sofie, I'll take you to the room. My brothers will be here shortly with the rest of your luggage," I tell the group.

I take Sofie's arm and lead her away from the ugly stares that follow us.

"Hey, wait a minute! Sofie and I are sharing a room!" Uppity Barbie wobbles after us in her ridiculous shoes.

Turning to face the disgruntled woman. I tell her, "The bride-to-be gets a room to herself, so if you'll excuse us." I turn and pull Sofie along with me, making her jog to keep up. The moment we step outside, I slow down. "Sorry about that. I figured you need some space."

She lets out a shaky breath. "Do I really have a room to myself?"

"Yes."

"Thank you so much. I wasn't sure how I'd manage sharing with her." She winces. "I shouldn't have said that."

I laugh and watch as her face lights with happiness. The first I've seen since she arrived although there was a split second when she alighted from the plane. "You can say whatever you want around me. Come on, you have one of the best suites. It's called Belle, from Beauty and the Beast."

Her eyes light up. "Really? I saw photographs on your website. It looked pretty."

"Mom had a hand in naming the bridal suites." I smirk. "We have two."

She snickers and twitches her pert nose as her eyes land on mine. "What's the other one named?" I watch her lick her lips, and my cock tries to punch its way out of my pants. I mentally tell it to behave.

I clear my throat and admit, "Rapunzel."

Her soft chuckle does something to me. I give her a side-long glance before ushering her toward the Belle Suite. "Here it is."

"Oh, it has a porch. This is amazing." She turns to face the snow-capped mountains in the distance. "That view is the reason I've always wanted to visit Alaska. I can't believe I'm here." Her excitement bubbles over, and she has me smiling along with her.

I guess that answers my question about why she chose Alaska for her bachelorette party. That thought snaps me back to the present. She's engaged to be married. That's why she's here. I need to remember that and rein in my arousal. If only my dick would behave!

I indicate for her to enter the room ahead of me. I'm so close that I hear the gasp leave her lips when she sees the room. I'm also close enough to smell the apple shampoo she uses on her hair. Since when do I care what shampoo a woman uses? Gah! I need to get out of here. But my feet have other ideas and I follow her inside.

The Belle Suite is a princess bedroom for adults. It has a canopy bed draped in sheer fabric, a crystal chandelier hanging from the ceiling, and plush velvet curtains framing the windows. I can't help but feel a surge of desire as I imagine her lying on the bed with her hair spread out around her like a halo. I push my desire to the back of my mind. I step forward to open the bathroom door.

The bathroom is just as luxurious as the bedroom, with marble countertops, a double vanity, and a rain shower. The room is filled with the scents of lavender and jasmine, creating a serene atmosphere that is perfect for relaxation. However, my mind is on other things when she brushes past me and leans over the tub in the center of the room. I close my eyes. Having her naked in the tub with me is a vivid fantasy that I can almost taste on my lips.

Snap out of it, Maddox, you horndog!

Sofie turns to face me, tears on her cheeks. Startled, I step into her space, cup her face, and wipe her tears away with my thumbs. "What is it?"

"This is the most gorgeous room I've ever seen. Are you sure I can stay here?"

"Usually, the bride-to-be stays in one of the suites. It's included in the bachelorette package. But whoever booked for you and your acquaintances obviously refused the suite."

"They did?" She sighs heavily and mutters, "That figures."

Uncertain what she means, I force myself to move toward the front door. "There's a sheet with numbers on in the drawer beneath the phone." I pause. "Can I see your phone?"

Frowning, she passes it over. I point the phone at her face to unlock it, then add my number and send myself a text. "You now have my number. Call if you need anything. It doesn't matter what time." I smile, tip my finger to my forehead, and leave, closing the door behind me.

The second I'm outside I let out a heavy breath and gaze off into the distance at the snow-capped peaks, concentrating on my breathing. I haven't gotten my dick wet in what feels like forever, so that must be why I feel a sudden attachment to the woman. It must be.

And she's getting married.

"Fuck!" I hiss under my breath as I head toward my cabin to retrieve my truck.

Chapter Four

Sofie

As soon as Maddox closes the door, I remove my jacket and kick off my boots before flopping down on the huge bed. I let out a sigh and find myself smiling as I look toward the doorway.

I'm engaged to be married even though I've decided to end things once I get home. But still. Having such an attraction to the big man is new. Exciting too. The way he looked at me made my panties wet and my body hum with arousal. What I do about it while Richard is still in the picture is a quandary.

I rub my temples, trying to shake off the negative feelings that are causing a headache. I'm prone to migraines, and the stress of this trip certainly hasn't helped. At least I'm no longer sharing a room with Samantha. I wish my friend Jamaica was here with me. Of course, Samantha was the reason why she wasn't.

My phone rings in my back pocket, but when I see the caller ID, I ignore it. It stops and starts up again. I glance at my watch to make sure I'm not late for the afternoon snacks and wine. Thankfully, I have plenty of time. My phone stops ringing, and I hold my breath, expecting Samantha to call again. It stays silent. Then it rings again. This time, Richard's name flashes on the screen.

I grind my teeth in annoyance but decide to answer the call. I stay silent and wait for him to speak.

"Sofie, are you there?"

"Yes, Richard. I'm here."

"Samantha told me that a beast of a man took you to a different room than the one she booked. She isn't happy with you. Neither is Mother. Who is this man?"

I need a moment to collect my thoughts because I really want to tell him to go fuck himself. Why have I allowed myself to become a doormat? "The man is one of the owners. Apparently, since I'm the bride-to-be, I get a suite. I'm not sharing it. I want my own space. End of story. Now, why are you calling me?"

"I can see you're in one of your moods. Is that why you're ignoring Samantha?"

"I was in the bathroom. Not that it's anyone's business. I'll see Samantha later. She has her friends with her to keep her company," I snap. "I'll talk to you later." I quickly hang up before he can say anything else or before I blurt out the truth —I don't love you. I can't marry you.

A few minutes later, my phone rings again—it's his mother! I send it to voicemail and quickly turn off my phone.

Peace at last.

I roll off the bed and cast a glare at my phone as I pick my jacket up from the floor and hang it on the built-in coat stand beside the door. The coat stand is quaint and reminds me of the country, with its overhead storage and bench for sitting while getting ready for the outdoors. I pad into the bathroom and smile once again when I see the luxurious room. The hot tub is calling my name, but I decide to explore the lodge and Hawkes Ridge for now. Hopefully, I can avoid the others.

I tug my boots onto my feet and decide to forgo my jacket because it's nice and warm outside. I open my suitcase and find a denim shirt to wear over my T-shirt. I leave my hair down, shove my sunglasses on top of my head, and, at the last minute, grab my phone.

Fresh air and the scent of flowers greet me as I step outside. I close the door behind me, checking the handle to make sure it's locked. Stepping off the porch, I tilt my face toward the sun, close my eyes, and enjoy the moment of being outside, away from blaring horns and foul smells like exhaust fumes and garbage in the city. There's no noise from people's loud chatter, either with friends or on their phones. It's totally peaceful.

When I open my eyes, I see a large structure directly ahead that makes me wonder if it houses the indoor pool. I follow the path through the garden and head up the steps, curious to find out. There is an abundance of well-kept flowers. I move toward what I assume to be the front of the building. I find it locked. A wooden sign beside the door indicates that I have found the pool, but it is closed.

"Hello there."

I turn around and find a man. A very handsome silver fox. He offers me a smile. "I didn't mean to startle you." He offers his hand. "Bryant Hawke."

Ah, this must be the father.

I smile and shake his hand. "Sofie Ryan."

"I know who you are," he says with a twinkle in his eye. "May I offer you a cup of coffee?"

"That would be lovely." I shuffle up beside him, letting him lead me away from the pool and up another path through a grove of trees. I catch my breath when we emerge on the other side. "Wow, these are gorgeous."

"Welcome to the cabins where my sons and I live. It's home. We call is Hawke Circle." He grins.

I glance around at the nine cabins grouped together. Each has a driveway large enough for a truck, and a few of them have one parked in the driveway. The wooden structures are identical, with a porch and a front door in the middle, and large windows on either side. There is a large circle of flowers in the middle of the cluster, which creates a turnaround for vehicles.

"This is really pretty."

Bryant chuckles. "My wife thinks it's wrong to live on the same street as my sons." He shrugs. "I haven't received a single complaint."

Feeling much lighter than before I met Bryant, I laugh and follow him up to the front porch of his cabin. Stepping inside, I see that it's rustic and gorgeous, with splashes of color from the throw blankets. "You are lucky to have such a lovely home."

"I am that. I would be even luckier if my wife decided to come home," he mutters sadly as he heads toward the kitchen.

I pause as I pass the table by the stairs, which is covered with photographs. "Are these your sons?"

He huffs out a laugh. "All eight of them," he says proudly.

"Your poor wife." I laugh.

"You'd really be saying that if you met her. She's tiny, and all the boys are over six feet tall, just like me." My eyes wander over the pictures but keep straying back to the one of Maddox. My belly tingles when I look at him.

Bryant clears his throat and adds, "That's Maddox, but you know that already." The twinkle is back in his eyes as I glance at him. "I invited you for coffee."

In the kitchen, I ask, "You said your wife isn't home yet?"

"She's a stubborn woman," he mutters as he brings out two mugs and sets them in front of me at the breakfast bar.

"She lives in Sugar Briar, Tennessee. She works for the mayor. There has been some trouble in town recently though, so maybe she will finally move here where her family is. Stubborn woman."

My eyes widen in surprise as he talks about his wife. "How long have you lived apart, if you don't mind me asking?"

"Ten years."

"Holy shit!" I slap a hand over my mouth. "I'm so sorry. That was rude of me."

"No need to apologize. I guess I'm stubborn, too." He pours coffee into our mugs and offers me creamer and sugar. I refuse and pick up my mug of black coffee. "I came out here to help a couple of my sons. It was supposed to be temporary. I never went home. I figured she'd follow me here. She hasn't yet. Now that our youngest son has been here a few months, I'm hoping she'll finally join me." He smirks. "I have a plan if she doesn't."

I watch him carefully and grin around my mug. "Are you going to go and collect her?"

"There might be some kidnapping involved, but she'll be living in Hawke's Ridge before the end of the year."

"You might want to get on the good side of the sheriff first if you're planning to kidnap her," I suggest. I feel at home talking to this man. I also see the family resemblance to Maddox.

He offers me a cookie from an open package and adds, "My oldest son is the sheriff." He grins. "He won't arrest me. After all, she's his mother, and we all want her here. She'd be here already if my sons would listen to me, find a woman, and put a bun in her oven. Louisa can never resist a baby, especially if it's her grandchild."

I splutter at his reference to putting a bun in her oven and laugh as I set my coffee mug down on a placemat. "So, none of your eight sons are married, huh? Why's that? What's wrong with them?"

"There's nothing wrong with us." A man whom I don't remember seeing before enters the cabin and pours himself some coffee. "Variety is the spice of life," he says with a wink my way.

"One of my sons, Spencer." Bryant frowns, and Spencer grins.

"And you are?" Spencer asks.

"It's none of your business," Bryant replies. "Maddox is sweet on her."

My cheeks heat and Spencer's eyebrows shoot up to his hairline. "Maddox?" He coughs. "No fucking way." Shaking his head, he sits beside me.

"Sofie Ryan," I say.

He smirks. "Ah, Colton told me about you."

"Colton?" *There's no way I'm going to remember all their names.*

"He checked you into the Lodge," he smiles.

"I remember him! I love the suite I'm in. It's stunning."

Spencer and Bryant exchange a look that I don't understand. I decide to leave them to discuss whatever it is that Spencer came to talk to his dad about. "Thank you for the coffee. I'm going to take a walk into town before I meet up with the others."

"Enjoy the fresh air," Spencer says.

Bryant accompanies me to the front door. "Have a good afternoon, and maybe we can have coffee again."

"I'd like that."

Chapter Five

Maddox

As I step out of the truck in town, I take a deep breath and inhale the scent of fresh flowers. I also hear the distant sound of laughter. The town is peaceful, especially during the winter, but we get quite a few tourists in the summer. Some stay at the Lodge, while others stay at one of the three bed and breakfasts in town or the few more scattered throughout nearby towns. The town's economy benefits greatly from tourism. Occasionally, we'll get ice fishermen who come in on one of the planes that land on the frozen lake during the winter.

Main Street is lined with quaint shops and cozy cafés that

cater to both locals and visitors. There's a strong sense of community here, and everyone comes together for events like the annual summer festival to name one.

If my great-great-great-grandfather were here today, I think he would be proud of how the town has changed since he made it his own with only a few other settlers back in the day.

Hopefully, future generations will continue to cherish and preserve this town's rich history.

Stepping onto the sidewalk, I enter the sheriff's station and find the front area busy. Four men and one woman are talking to Deputy Landon, all with concerned expressions. I recognize them as guests of the Lavender B&B who have been in town for a couple of days.

Landon glances my way, his eyes begging for an intervention. He seems overwhelmed by the crowd, so I step behind the desk to help defuse the situation. "Can I help?"

"Are you the sheriff?" the older man in the group asks.

I shake my head. "No, that would be my brother. What seems to be the issue? Maybe I can help."

A woman, early twenties, steps forward. "I'm Olivia Denver and this is my dad, Peter, and brothers, Scott, Jason, and Lyle," briefly pausing she continues, "I saw someone lurking suspiciously behind the B&B last night. The person was huge and had a knife in one hand. It was freaky." The woman said, her expression worried. "I was on the back porch getting some air before bed. I ran inside, went to my room, and looked out the window. The man was staring up at me. I'm scared, okay?"

I frown. "I can see that. Give me a minute to talk with my brother. If he's busy, I'll accompany Deputy Landon to the B&B and check out the area." Landon sighs. The lazy ass can do some work for a change. "Where's the sheriff?" I ask him.

Landon waves behind him, so I head toward my brother's office. He's the oldest, and if you don't know him, you'd think he was a grumpy old man. But he's a teddy bear really—not that I'll ever let him hear me call him that. I like my face too much.

I knock on his door and waltz right in, only to be greeted with a dark stare. I raise an eyebrow. "What'd you find in your cereal this morning?"

He gives me the finger as I slump into the chair opposite his desk. "Prowler report at the back of Lavender B&B. A woman and her family are out front making a report. I said I'd check it out with Landon if you're busy."

He nods.

I rub a hand over my jaw and hold my brother's gaze. "The girl says she saw him from the back porch. He was huge and had a knife. She ran inside to her room and looked out the window. The guy was staring up at her. It freaked her out."

Branson grunts. "Landon can stay here. You can come with me." He stands and grabs his hat from the coatrack. "This is the second report I've had about a prowler. Herbert Merryfield reported seeing a large man at the back of his property night before last."

"Well, shit." I follow my brother out of the room to where the family is waiting. I stand back while he introduces himself and sends the family on their way.

"I'll follow you down the street." I wince. "Betty won't be happy with us trampling around the back of her B&B."

"She'll be fine."

I snicker. "She still has a crush on you, huh?"

"Don't push it, asshole!" He pauses and asks, "Is there an issue up at the lodge?"

"No." I climb into my truck and wait for my brother to get his vehicle turned around before following him to the outskirts of town. I try not to be irritated that my brother thinks I would only visit him if there were trouble. I'm still upset about it when I climb out of my vehicle. I stride over to his door, yank it open, and startle him. "You're my brother! There doesn't need to be trouble for me to come see you!"

I stomp around to the back of the B&B, a three-story brick building, the front clad in wood. It's painted lavender with white trim. I'm not particularly into decorating, but since we built the lodge, I've noticed things whether I want to or not.

Branson catches up to me and, after giving me the eye, moves forward. We tread carefully so as not to disrupt any footprints that might have been left behind. "Did you find anything at Merryfield's place?"

"Size fifteen boot prints."

"So, we're looking for Bigfoot, then?"

I keep my head down, scanning the area, as Branson

shoots a dark glare over his shoulder. My brother never smiles and ignores stupid shit.

"Fuck," he curses under his breath. My head shoots up, and my eyes follow his line of sight. About five feet in front of him, there is a large pool of blood, only noticeable because it's covering pale leaves.

"It could be from an animal," I suggest, even though there's a lot of blood not to have the dead animal here as well.

"Something was butchered here." Branson turns to face me and holds my gaze. "I don't like the look of this." He huffs out a breath. "I have some precipitin tests in the truck. Let me go get one to see what we're dealing with." He winces. "I hope it isn't human blood."

"I'll wait." I pause. "I won't trample your crime scene."

"It's not going to be a crime scene," he grumbles as he trudges away.

I slowly survey the area, checking for movement or anything unusual. Nothing catches my eye. The area back here is wild and untamed, with looming trees casting eerie shadows on the ground. When Branson returns with the test kit, I can't shake the feeling that we're not alone.

"Bro, don't react, but I have this feeling we're being watched," I whisper.

"I sense it too." Branson crouches at the edge of the blood and fiddles with the kit in his hands. After about a minute, he curses wildly and stands up. His face is stone-cold as he slowly turns and looks deep into the forest. "It's human," he grinds out. Meeting my gaze, he adds, "I need to call this into Anchorage. I need a crime scene team out here."

"Want me to keep going?" I ask.

"I moved here for peace and quiet. I fucking hate seeing death."

I wince. "You don't know that we'll find a body."

He gives me a dark look, which makes me feel like I'm grasping at thin air. "There's too much blood for there not to be one." He sighs and looks off into the trees. "I'll go straight ahead." He hands me some orange flags. "Head in and move alongside but stay about five feet from me."

"Got it." We've only gone a few steps when I shout, "Got something!" I put a flag on the ground and step around what looks like a partial boot impression.

After a few more steps, Branson shouts and places a flag. I wince at the mess I suspect my brother is going to have to deal with. He quit his job as a homicide detective in Boston six years ago to escape the gruesome scenes that sucked the life out of him. Now, he has one here.

Neither of us has anything to shout about until I hear my brother curse. He doesn't stop with just a few curse words. "Bro, over here."

"If you've found a body, I don't want to see it," I tell him.

"Stop being a pussy and get your ass over here."

He's found a body.

"Fuck!" I hiss at the sight. "Bro, not cool."

"Get over it." He snaps. "Do you recognize her? She looks familiar."

The poor woman is hanging from a thick branch by a rope around her neck. I force myself to look at her face, distorted by death. I glance away, not wanting to see her like that. Something about that quick glimpse triggers a memory, and I feel all the blood drain from my head. "Andrea," I whisper. "Gabe dated her a few times, but she skipped town."

"I don't think she skipped anywhere," Branson comments. "Can you get Hunter down here? Tell him I need him as my deputy."

"Sure." I turn my back on the poor woman while tugging my cell phone out of my jeans pocket. I freeze. Movement to the left pulls my gaze, but whatever I saw has disappeared. I frown, wondering if it was human or animal. *There!* "Fuck! Person in the trees!" I take off toward where I last saw them, Branson's heavy footsteps behind me.

As I push through the dense undergrowth, I catch a glimpse of a figure disappearing into the shadows. With adrenaline coursing through my veins, I head in that direction. When I arrive, I don't see anyone. Branson and I stand back-to-back. He has his weapon drawn. There is no visual or sound of anyone nearby.

"Text Hunter," Branson orders.

Keeping my eyes and ears open, I quickly shoot our brother a message. He replies that he's on his way.

"Whoever was here is gone now." Branson holsters his weapon and steps in beside me as we head back to the body. "We need to tell Gabe."

"I'll head back when reinforcements show up and tell him

then." I pause, taken aback by the sight of the poor woman. "Wait, shouldn't she smell?"

Branson glances my way and frowns. "I only smell the forest and the tinge of blood." He watches his steps as he moves toward Andrea. He sniffs. "She smells of ice. I think she's been frozen."

"Hell." I take a step back.

Branson grunts. "Our victim is frozen, so where the fuck has the blood come from?"

"Or who," I add on a sigh. "Is Landon coming?" I just want to get the fuck out of here. Branson's job fucking sucks.

"I sent him a message." Branson moves closer and puts his hands on his utility belt. "When Landon and Hunter get here, you head out. I'd rather you not be here when the crime scene unit arrives."

I wince. "I can handle Janice. You need me here."

"Since you slept with her, she's been a bitch to me. So no, I do not want you here when she arrives."

I clench my jaw and snap, "I didn't fuck her! She wanted me to. Threw herself at me, and she got angry when I refused. I've told you this. It's about time you listened to me." I stomp off, trying to follow my footprints back to the B&B. "I'll wait for Landon or Hunter to arrive before I leave," I shout over my shoulder.

I'm irritated with him, but there's no way I'd leave him here alone.

Chapter Six

Sofie

On my way through the small garden, I take my time because the peace and quiet are truly welcome. The fresh air, too. It's something I can't get enough of. I pause to stare at the snow-capped mountains in the distance and feel grateful for this tranquil moment in nature.

The sound of someone hurrying toward me draws my gaze. I smile when I notice Spencer approaching. He looks apprehensive. "Everything okay?" I ask.

He runs a hand through his hair. "Maddox called as you left. He freaked out when I told him you were on your way into town." He winces. "He was with our brother, the sheriff, when they found a woman's body."

"Oh, the poor woman." I cover my mouth, feeling slightly off-kilter at the news. It's scary to hear news like that in such a small town.

Spencer shoves his hands on his hips, stares off into the distance, and then his gaze lands on me. "I'm glad I wasn't there. Maybe you should stay at the lodge for now. We wouldn't want you to be in any danger."

"What?"

"I didn't mean to scare you. It happened overnight. I just mean that there's no chance you'll see anything if you're here. Maddox will be back soon."

My ears certainly perk up at the mention of Maddox. Then I remember that he and his brother found the body. "Maddox is okay, right?" I know I shouldn't be concerned, but I am. I don't care if he knows that. Not after the horror he's probably seen.

Spencer hesitates. "He's fine. He'll be back soon. He's waiting for Deputy Landon to arrive so he can leave. Another one of our brothers is also a deputy, so Hunter is on his way, too." He reaches out and gently rubs my arm. "Maddox is fine." Offering me a wry smile, he adds, "I need to get going."

"Okay. Thanks for telling me."

As he takes a few steps away, I think for a moment, then ask, "Spencer, why does everyone keep—well—" I blush, unsure of how to ask what I want to know.

It turns out Spencer knows what I'm asking. "There are

eight of us. All it took was one text message for us all to know about you." He winks and continues on his way.

My cheeks feel heated as I quickly get moving. Glancing at my watch, I see that I still have time for a walk. Despite having been told what's going on, I decide to head into town. I don't want to stay at the lodge and possibly run into the others in my group.

I know I should, and it makes me sad that I don't feel comfortable around them. If they didn't constantly criticize me, it would be different. I'm a strong person and have never had issues speaking out. But, to keep the peace, I've kept my mouth shut. It's wearing on me at this point.

When I reach the road, I turn right and find myself on the main street through town. I don't reach for my phone to take pictures. I can do that another day. Right now, I just want to experience Hawke's Ridge, with its picturesque storefronts, rocking chairs on porches, and abundance of flowers. Fancy trees with ball-shaped branches and leaves line the sidewalk every ten feet or so. The town is clean and fresh that a smile lights my face as I peer into a candy store. My stomach rumbles, reminding me that I haven't eaten since an early breakfast before we left San Francisco.

The Cessna flight had been interesting and noisy. Richard's father wanted to contribute to the trip, so he booked the private flight. You'd think he would have booked it for later in the day, though. I wince. I sound ungrateful, but I'm not. I mean, I'm here in Alaska.

Coming out of my own head, I take a deep breath and

inhale the scent of the flowery blooms in the hanging basket beside me. The crisp air bites my skin, reminding me that it's getting late. It's time to head back to the lodge and leave the beautiful scenery behind. I sigh heavily and turn to check the traffic before crossing, and startle when a vehicle brakes hard, its tires screeching.

I gasp when Maddox emerges from the truck, looking less than thrilled to see me. I take a step back and find myself backed up against a storefront. Maddox crowds me, caging me in with his arms as he presses close. My heart pounds in my chest. I'm unsure of what he's going to do next but secretly hope he's going to kiss me. "I told Spencer to keep you at the lodge," he growls. His voice is low, dangerous, and oh so sexy.

My body is tight and swollen with anticipation, which scares me in a way because I haven't told Richard we're over. "Oh!" I gasp and push against his chest, but he doesn't budge. "You can't be this close to me. We can't do this." My voice doesn't sound like my own. It's husky and filled with need.

"Sofie," he whispers.

My eyes lift to his, and I'm frozen in time. "Why do I have this nearly irresistible urge to throw myself into your arms and beg you to fuck me?" I whisper, surprising myself. His eyes narrow, darkening with arousal. "We met mere hours ago, yet when I look at you or you touch me, my body swells, and my hooha gets wet and tingly. I shouldn't feel like this for you," I finish, my voice barely audible.

His eyes blaze with fire as he dips his face into my neck and whispers, "You can feel how hard you make me." He suckles my pulse point, and my legs go weak. I grasp hold of him, digging my fingertips into his side. He shudders. "Your confession has me pulsing and leaking precum into my jeans." He nibbles my earlobe while I let out a soft moan. His breath feels as heavy as mine. His searching mouth moves to the corner of mine. His eyes meet mine as he presses a kiss there, sending shivers down my spine. "How wet is your *hooha* now?" His eyes dance with mirth.

I offer a soft smile. "My *hooha* has never been wetter, nor has it ever ached like it does now."

"Fuck," he curses, dropping his forehead to mine while keeping our eyes locked. "If we weren't on Main Street, I'd shove my hand in your jeans, finger-fuck you, and then lick my fingers clean."

"Oh!" I whimper, clinging to him. "Maddox, this is wrong," I gasp.

"It feels perfect to me." His lips brush over mine, and then he takes a deep breath before pulling away. He takes my hand and leads me around to the passenger seat of his truck, lifting me inside.

I flop back against the seat, wondering what just happened. What is it about this man that makes me want to jump him?

He joins me in the cab, leans over, and snaps my seatbelt into place. "Spencer," I say, wanting to move on from a few moments ago. "He told me you and your brother found a dead woman. Are you okay?"

Maddox winces and holds out his hand for mine. I smile

and take his hand, intertwining our fingers. "I feel better for seeing you." He kisses my knuckles and then gets the truck moving. "It was bad. I recognized her. She'd been in town for a year or so. I wish I could unsee it."

"I'm sorry, Maddox. That must have been awful." He pulls into the lodge, and I don't want to leave him while he's upset, but I don't think I have a choice. "This is bad timing, but I need to head back and change. Samantha has wine and hors d'oeuvres planned." I face him. "I want to stay with you."

"I'll be okay." He tugs on my hand. "You have things planned with the others. It's fine." He smiles, leans forward, and kisses me on the cheek. "It's as well that you're not staying, because I want you wrapped around me."

I sigh and softly admit, "I'd like that." I pull back and offer him a wry smile, adding, "I love this place. It's peaceful, and it's away from everything."

"It is." He clears his throat and says, "I'll walk you back," and releases my hand.

Chapter Seven

Maddox

I REST MY HANDS ON THE BREAKFAST BAR AND concentrate on breathing, wondering what the hell I'm doing. There's no denying my connection with Sofie, but she's engaged. *"She isn't married yet,"* a little voice whispers in the back of my mind. I briefly met her future mother-in-law and sister-in-law, and I don't think much of them. Well, that's not entirely true. I think they're both bitches. This makes me wonder what her fiancé is like. Is he like his mom and sister? "Fuck," I shout in frustration.

"I'd sleep with her and get her out of my system."

My head snaps toward the doorway where my dad and my brother Garrett stand.

"How long have you been there?"

Garrett snickers. "Long enough to know you're fighting with yourself."

Dad moves forward and pats me on the arm. "She isn't happy, Maddox." He fills the kettle with water and lights the burner.

"How do you know she's unhappy?" I sit and let him get on with what he's doing. Over the years, I've learned that letting him get it out sooner rather than later saves me a headache. Garrett sits at the end of the counter.

"I read it in her coffee leaves." Dad smirks.

"You only use instant coffee."

"Okay, genius." He dumps tea bags into three cups, making me wince.

I hate tea. I glance at my brother and notice the wince on his face. He rolls his eyes when he catches my gaze.

"I can see you both. Tea ends all troubles," says Dad.

"Who told you that?" Garrett mumbles.

Dad turns and grins. "Your mother."

"Ouch," I say, laughing.

Dad waves the teaspoon in my face. "We'll have a cup of tea and call your mother. She'll tell you how to convince Sofie to stay here with you!" He smirks. "It doesn't have to be with you, mind you. You have seven brothers who also need wives."

"My brothers better not look at my woman," I growl, shooting a glare down the counter at Garrett.

"Hey, you know we don't poach," Garrett replies, offended.

"Look," I sigh. "I don't think calling Mom right now is a good idea. Besides, I don't want to mess anything up for Sofie. She might love the guy."

Dad snorts. "Spencer told me she was worried about you when he told her what you found with Branson. That girl has eyes for you. That wouldn't happen if she were happy."

She wants me to fuck her.

I shove the thought away and huff. "We're acting like a bunch of girls."

Dad shoves a cup of tea into my hands. I peer at the steaming liquid and find I'm relieved to see that he left it black.

Not thirty seconds later, I hear Mom's voice coming through the speaker. Garrett laughs and wraps an arm around my neck. He drags me over to where Dad sits at the small dining table.

"And there are two of my boys," Mom sighs, a huge smile on her face.

"You'll see all eight of your boys when you move out here," I tell her.

"Oh, poppycock." She scoffs. "There's been so much fun here. Tallulah James arranged a murder mystery reveal on a party boat. You remember her, right? She went to school with Spencer. Oh, there were so many shenanigans."

Mom is thrilled by all this news, and my mind boggles.

"All I can think about right now is how the fuck a party boat works in Sugar Briar," I mutter.

"Watch your mouth," Mom chides. "There's a big lake outside Sugar Briar. The boat runs on that. It's been rather popular. Of course, after the shenanigans, it's fully booked for a while." Mom shudders.

Before she can start talking again, Dad jumps in, "Maddox has a girl." He's blunt and to the point.

Her mouth drops open, and I wince at the look on her face.

"I do not have a girl," I counter.

"He wants a girl," Garrett adds. "You need to come here and help him out. I mean, you want grandkids, right?"

"That's right, babe," Dad says. "Sofie and Maddox need a woman's touch. The poor girl is going to be miserable if she marries her fiancé, so she needs help. So, you see, your son needs you."

Her eyes narrow. "Is this a ploy to get me to Alaska?"

"Here it is," I say. "Sofie Ryan arrived a few hours ago. I felt an immediate connection with her, and she did too. She's one of eleven in a bachelorette party. It's her party. The groom's mother and sister are bitches. I'm not sure where she belongs, but it's not with him!"

"Maddox Jameson Hawke, you're not too old to have your mouth rinsed out with soap!" Mom snaps. "I'll book a flight." The line goes dead.

The three of us stare at the black phone, wondering if we heard her right.

"Did Mom just say she was booking a flight?" Colton asks, breaking the silence.

I turn to face my youngest brother and nod. "Yeah, she did."

He scoffs. "I told Dad to pretend that another woman was after him, and that he needed her to come over and chase her off. He wouldn't have it. She would have been here already if he had."

"I'm not lying to your mother." He frowns. "I thought you were scheduled to work the reception until eight?"

"I'm taking a break before Branson arrests me for killing a guest." He flops onto my sofa, head at one end and feet hanging off the other. "Those women you brought earlier are a pain in the ass. The older one especially." He groans and sighs. "Is Mom really coming here? No bullshit."

"You heard her," I say. "Why do you want to murder a guest?"

"Catherine Walker has called not once or twice, but twelve times looking for her daughter." He drops his feet to the floor, sits forward, and eyes us. "First, she wanted Sofie's room number. I refused to give it to her and quoted the lodge privacy policy. Then, she wanted someone to go to Sofie's room and tell her to return her call. I figured Sofie had the good sense to ignore her. I wish I could do the same." He rubs a hand down his face. "I can't wait for them to check out."

I rub my brows and ask, "Why is everyone in my cabin?"

"Bro, I'll end up falling asleep if I go to mine," Colton says.

"You can come to mine. I'll feed you before you go back to work," Dad says.

"Ugh," Colton moans as he shoves up and gives Garrett and me the finger behind Dad's back.

Ignoring my youngest sibling, I ask Garrett, "Do you know where Gabe is?"

"Fiddling with one of the hot tubs. At least he was when I came over."

"I need to talk to him." I head to the front door, and Garrett follows.

"Want company?"

I eye him. "Sure."

"What's going on in town?"

"Found a dead body behind the Lavender B&B."

"I know that. Did you recognize her?"

"Maybe."

He grabs my arm and turns me to face him. "Who is it?"

"Wait until we get to Gabe, so I don't have to repeat myself."

His eyes widen. "Oh, shit! It's that Andrea chick, isn't it? Fuck!"

"You know her?" I cross my arms over my chest, wondering where this is going. "Because I thought Gabe dated her."

"He did, so get that idea right out of your head," he snaps. "Gabe complained to me on and off about Andrea leaving when she was talking about moving into his cabin with him. He tried to find her, but he had no luck."

"Shit," I say, starting to move again. "I didn't know they were that serious."

"Honestly, I think she was. You know what he's like. I also don't think he tried all that hard to find her."

"Fuck!"

"Why do you two look like your best friend died?" Gabe jokes as he sees us approaching. He's searching through an assortment of nuts and bolts in front of him.

"Maddox found someone you lost," Garrett says, pissing me off.

I shoot him a glare, and he shrugs. Gabe frowns between us. I just go with it. "Andrea didn't leave town, Gabe. She's the woman Branson and I found."

"What are you talking about?" He drops his tools and stands. "What woman?"

"We found Andrea behind one of the B&Bs in town. She'd been frozen, and then—" I pause, not wanting to conjure that image in his mind. Being in mine was bad enough.

"Go on," he says quietly, dropping his butt onto the bench.

"Remember that she was already dead, okay? We found her hanging from a tree. Branson has no clue how she died because it wasn't obvious with her being frozen and all." I wipe a hand down my face. "I didn't want you to hear it from someone else."

"I thought she left because I wasn't keen on her moving in with me." He winces. "I tried to find her for answers, but I didn't put much effort into it to be honest. Now, I feel like a bastard." He stands and faces the mountains. "I need to be alone." Over his shoulder, he says, "That needs repairing. Two of the nozzles are blocked."

"What a fucking mess." Garrett gets down and searches through the tools. "You go do whatever you need to do. I've got this."

"I need a shower and food."

Chapter Eight

Sofie

My nerves are all aflutter after having Maddox pressed against me. He was hard and delicious, and I wanted nothing more than to take off my clothes and tell him to take me. I swallow hard, pressing a hand to my stomach, and move to stand in front of the mirror in my room. I look pretty in my navy-blue cocktail dress. The chiffon sleeves fasten around my wrists, and the dress fits my curves nicely. The navy pumps on my feet give me height and make my legs look amazing.

My mind wanders back to Maddox, and I wonder if he'll get to see me all dressed up. My hair, freshly washed, is styled into curls that fall down my back. A light coating of makeup covers my face. As my diamond engagement ring catches the light, my heart drops. What am I doing? I step close and let my forehead drop. The cool glass against my skin does nothing to settle me.

I haven't even spent a day in Hawke's Ridge, and yet I'm already questioning my future. To be honest, I started feeling unsettled with Richard about a month ago if not longer. It wasn't just one thing. It was as though a light had suddenly switched on in my head, opening my eyes. I saw how Richard manipulates me into thinking his way. I'd just agree with him because I don't like arguing. Looking at my reflection, I wonder if these negative feelings about Richard and his family are a reaction to Maddox. Or maybe meeting Maddox has opened my eyes to the fact that deep down, I don't want to become Mrs. Richard Walker.

Stepping back, I straighten and inhale before slowly exhaling. "I'm Sofie Ryan, and from this point forward, I will not be a doormat to the Walkers!" I huff out a breath and retrieve my purse, making sure my phone is inside. Once I step outside, I put the keycard inside my bag. A smile plays on my lips as I glance around and notice that there is still daylight. From what I've read, the sun usually doesn't set until around eleven in the evening and rises again after two in the morning. That explains the blackout curtains in the room.

I take my time, meandering along the stone pathways that lead to the main building. My stomach grumbles, reminding me that I haven't eaten in a while. I hope there's more than cheese at this event Samantha organized.

Inside the building, I see the others standing and talking in the bar area. It would have been good to have Jamaica with me about now.

"Sofie, may I accompany you to the bar?" Colton Hawke offers me his arm.

Flustered, I slip my arm through his and whisper, "Thank you," as he leads me forward. "It's like being led into a room of snakes."

He huffs a laugh his eyes dancing. "Don't worry. The Hawke men have you covered."

I glance at the young man and laugh when he winks.

"Now, what can I get you to drink?" He asks.

"I'd love a whiskey. Wine isn't going to cut it tonight."

He snorts. "I wish I could join you." He releases me. "Ice?"

"Please."

He groans, his eyes focusing on something over my shoulder. I turn to see what has his attention and let out a small groan.

"I'll get you a double," Colton mutters as he moves away.

"Where have you been?" Catherine snaps the second Colton is out of earshot.

She reaches out and grabs my arm, her nails digging into my skin like talons. I narrow my eyes and hiss, "Take your hands off me right now, or we are going to have a big problem."

"Don't be ridiculous." She huffs.

I try to wrench my arm free, but she clings tightly. What the hell is she doing?

"Ma'am, I suggest you release Miss. Ryan." Spencer peels her fingers from my arm and gently takes my elbow to move me out of her reach. "The sheriff takes issue with physical abuse."

"Well, really!" She gasps. "I was just being friendly to my future daughter-in-law." Her eyes narrow as Samantha joins us.

She lets her gaze pass over the three of us and then settles it on me. "Sofie, are you causing problems again?"

"Fuck this!" I snap, turning to Spencer. "Thank you. I need a drink."

"I have it right here." Colton hands me a glass of whiskey. I take a long sip, enjoying the burn as it goes down.

"Thank you."

"Will you be okay if I leave?" Spencer asks in a quiet voice.

"I'll be fine." I smile. "I plan on getting drunk. Then all my problems will disappear." I turn and head for the bar. On my way, I spot a table with hors d'oeuvres. I walk over, load up a small plate, and then go sit at the bar. A man steps out from behind the bar, surprising me. He grins. "Hello, Sofie. In case you're wondering, I'm the better-looking brother, Ryland Hawke."

"The Hawke men are all incorrigible." I wave a finger his way. "Could you please get me another one of these? Colton got me this one."

"Sure can."

I start munching on a chicken curry kebab and a pastry, but I can't really taste them. The round things on a stick are delicious. This food isn't going to sustain me until morning.

When Ryland returns with my drink, I ask, "Did they order food for tonight?"

He shakes his head. "I heard them talking. They only booked snacks."

"Well, that sucks. I'm starving." I finish one drink and pick up the next. I wave it in the air. "Bottoms up!"

I sense a presence on my right, glance that way, and see a woman whose name escapes me. She's one of Samantha's friends. Well, they all are.

"I'm Judean." She smiles. "I'm kind of an 'invite when you need a space filler' friend of Samantha's."

I wince. "That sucks." I wave my glass toward Ryland. "Could my friend have one of these, please, and could I have another one?"

"So, Judean—I love your name by the way—how do you know Samantha?" I ask, starting to feel a buzz from the alcohol.

"School." She takes a sip of the drink Ryland places in front of her. "Samantha wanted ten people on the trip, her mom number eleven. She was adamant that we all share rooms, except for Catherine." She shrugs. "It's a free trip, so I thought, 'Why not?' The company could have been nicer. I do wonder why you would marry into the Walker family, though."

"I'm wondering that as well," I mutter, just as my stomach rumbles loudly.

"You're as hungry as I am. Do you want to sneak away and find some real food?"

"Judean, I think I would love that!"

I slide off the barstool and wobble slightly on my heels, wondering if I'm going to fall flat on my face when I try to walk.

Ryland huffs out a laugh. "Ladies, if you want a burger and fries, I can help you out."

"You have our attention," Judean says.

"Follow me." Ryland leads us behind the bar and down a hallway until we burst into a huge kitchen.

Judean stops suddenly, and I bump into her as I hurry to the food. It has nothing to do with the three double whiskeys I just consumed. "Um, do the men come with the food?" Judean asks in a loud whisper directed at Ryland.

Ryland snorts. "Ladies, meet my brothers: Maddox, Hunter, Garrett, and Gabe. Bros, these ladies are hungry."

"Good thing we're cooking up some burgers," Maddox drawls as he moves toward me.

I meet him halfway, giving him a drunken grin as I wrap my arms around his waist. "You smell good."

He chuckles. "You look hot." He squeezes my butt and pushes me away. "How much have you had to drink?"

"Three."

"Three double Jack and Cokes," Ryland shouts.

"Fuck!" Maddox walks me backward and then grabs my hips, plopping my butt down on the table. "Stay there while I make you food."

"Okay." I sigh, staring at the nice, firm backside in front of me.

Maddox chuckles when he catches me staring. "Behave."

"I think I need an ice-cold bath," Judean says beside me. "The man who had his hands all over you is hot." She nudges me with her elbow and whispers, "Who is that?" She's not quiet at all, and all heads swivel toward who she's looking at.

I frown, not recognizing the man who just entered.

"Um," Gabe snickers. "That would be our brother, Branson."

He is as tall as his brothers, but he wears a more serious expression. Then I remember that he's the sheriff. I wiggle down from the table, walking slowly so as not to make a fool of myself, and continue until I'm right in front of him. "Hello, Branson. I'm Sofie, and this is my new friend, Judean." I smile. "You look tired and hungry. Your brothers are making food." I grab his arm, lead him to the table, and push him into a seat. "Are you okay? I know you've had a bad day."

Branson glances at his brothers, shakes his head, and lets out a long sigh. "It's been a long time since I came home to a woman."

"Asshole. She's mine." Maddox sets plates of food on the table and motions for me to sit in the chair across from his brother. Judean dives into her food, her eyes riveted on the men. Maddox grabs a plate for himself and sits next to me, making sure our thighs press together.

Branson keeps his eyes on us while he eats, his lips twitching. Maddox nudges my plate closer, and I decide to dig in. Breakfast was a long time ago.

Chapter Nine

Maddox

"So," Sofie says, waving a fry toward Branson with a delicate hand. He raises a brow, clearly amused. "You're the eldest, right? That means you have more insight into your brothers. I want to know why none of you are married."

A few snorts fill the silence while Branson shuffles in his chair, clearly uncomfortable with the question. I could help him out, but I decide to stay quiet and hear what he has to say. After clearing his throat a few times, he shoots me a dark look before softening his gaze as he stares at Sofie. "We haven't met the right woman yet."

"Huh, well, I have a friend. She'd love you. Her name's

Jamaica, and she would be a comfort to come home to. She's feisty as well. So, plenty of excitement in the sack!" She smirks. "I'm going to tell her about you."

I try to muffle a laugh, but Branson shoots me a nasty look before turning it on our brothers. He hears our amusement and curses under his breath. He points his fork at Sofie, then at me. "Your woman needs to sleep it off."

"Are you insinuating that I'm drunk?" Sofie asks, glancing around. "Where'd my burger and fries go?"

Judean snorts. "You ate it. That hunky guy took your plate away while you were grilling the sheriff."

"That doesn't help. They're all hunky."

My brothers nudge each other and laugh. I stand. "Let's get you to bed."

"Are you coming with me?" she asks, batting her eyelashes.

Ignoring my amused brothers, I say, "I'll tuck you in."

"I want someone to tuck me in!" Her friend Judean complains.

"Don't worry, babe. I'll tuck you in."

"Have we met before?" Judean asks.

"I'm Colton Hawke, at your service," he tells her. She practically floats toward my youngest brother.

"You're a bit young for me. Do you even know what to do with it?" Judean stumbles, but Colton steadies her.

Our brothers laugh their heads off, and even Branson chuckles. Colton gives them the finger as he wraps an arm around Judean's waist. "Babe, I can assure you that I know exactly what to do with it."

"I bet you could teach him a thing or two," Sofie mumbles as I pull her close, wanting to teach her a few things.

"Sofie, let's just get you to bed so you can sleep." As we move out onto the deck, I hear a whiny voice wondering where Sofie and Judean have gone. I steer Sofie in the opposite direction and pick up speed before we're caught. Hidden behind the bushes on one of the small pathways, I glance at Sofie, who lets out a sigh.

"I think I'm okay now. Food and fresh air always help me feel better."

"Do you get drunk often?"

She gives a very unladylike snort. "I hardly ever get drunk. I needed some Dutch courage to be surrounded by piranhas." She grins at me. "I think I like Judean. She told me she's the one who gets invited to events just to fill up the guest list." She scrunches her nose. "That's kind of sad."

"Maybe you have a friend in her."

"I'd like that." She pauses. "It really is beautiful here."

I agree, but I remain silent as she stares off into the distance, lost in thought. This has been my home for almost ten years. I can't imagine living elsewhere. I've built my life here, and I'm content. The woman in my arms slowly leads me further along the path to her suite. It's a small cabin set back from the main part of the lodge, behind the landscaped pathways. It's private, and I hope her snooping soon-to-be family members won't find it at least not for a day or two.

"I like how you and your brothers interact. It's sweet."

I chuckle and pull her into my body, wrapping an arm around her neck. "Sometimes it's sweet. Sometimes it's a war zone," I reply, kissing her forehead.

She sighs, hugs me, and rests her head on my chest. I swallow hard, feeling a surge of protectiveness wash over me. "This is me," she says softly. "Do you want to come inside?"

My heart suddenly races, then calms. "Sofie, if I come in with you, I'm going to spend the night making love to you." I cup her face. "You're still engaged, and you'd feel guilty in the morning, plus I wouldn't let you go." Resting my forehead gently against hers, I whisper, "When we're together, I don't want you to have any regrets."

Tears hover on her lashes as she struggles to control her emotions. "I haven't been here a day. This instant connection with you scares me, Maddox. Yet at the same time, I feel exhilarated."

I kiss each of her eyelids and force myself to step away. "I'm not going anywhere." I pull her back into my arms, holding her close as I rest my chin on the top of her head. I could hold Sofie like this for a long time. She gives me peace, even though my body reacts to her. She isn't mine and holding her like this is the closest I'll allow myself to get right now.

"I should get to bed," she says, yawning.

"Bed sounds good." I squeeze her one last time before releasing her. She smiles and hesitates for a moment before turning and entering her room.

Looking out toward the mountains, I look up at the sky

and exhale loudly. Sofie Ryan has been sent here to tempt me like no other woman. I chuckle and shake my head as I head toward the family cabins.

As I head through the tunnel of kissing trees, Branson steps out of the shadows and walks with me, slowing my pace, knowing he wants to talk. "I like her," he says. "Not so much the people she's with."

I frown. "You met the group?"

He huffs out a laugh. "I was ambushed as soon as I stepped inside the resort. You'd think they'd never seen a cop before."

I snicker. "You're the only man I know who wouldn't like being ambushed by a group of women."

"One of them reached for my crotch, so I grabbed her wrist and told her I'd arrest her for molesting a cop." He grins. "She went bright red and fled back to the bar. The older woman apologized and asked if I were a real cop." He narrows his eyes. "They thought I was a stripper!" he mumbles.

I can't help myself and burst out laughing. Okay, maybe I howl with laughter. My brother gives me such a dark glare that I force myself to stop, which isn't easy. Still snickering, I ask, "What did you do?"

"I shot them all a glare, pushed my way through them, and escaped to the kitchen." He shudders. "The older one trailed behind me, wanting to know if I could find her daughter-in-law, who has disappeared. It took me a minute to realize she referred to Sofie."

Heaving a heavy sigh, I glance back toward where Sofie

should be tucked in bed, but I force myself to stay with my brother. I face him. "What's happening with the case?"

He searches my gaze for a moment before answering, "The team arrived and called it a night, which is why I made it here." He runs a hand through his dark hair. "The blood found is the same type as the victim's. We need a DNA analysis to confirm the match, though. The time of death is impossible to determine because she's been frozen. Nothing else was found in the searched area. The only thing I can do tomorrow is go back and question everyone who knew her."

"Have you spoken to Gabe?" I ask.

"He feels guilty for not trying harder to find her."

"I know. It sounds like he was glad she left. He used to meet up with her and her friends, so he should be able to give you names."

"He's writing down everything he remembers about her. About her family and friends. I'm meeting him for breakfast."

"Good. Let me know how he's doing."

"Sure," he sighs. "I'm going to get some sleep." He trudges off toward his cabin while I make my way to mine.

Chapter Ten

Sofie

I'm about to head out to look for breakfast when I hear Catherine and Samantha directly outside. I plaster myself against the front door of my cabin.

A loud knock makes me jump, but I don't move. My heart pounds heavily in my chest and blood rushes through my ears. I can't hear them, but I sense they haven't left. I kept the curtains closed and, luckily, but the lights were off. Two more rapid knocks make me flinch.

"Mom, she's in there!" An angry Samantha says.

"You don't know that. There are no lights on."

"How would we know that? They're blackout curtains," Samantha huffs.

She's right, too. I can't see daylight with the curtains drawn, so they can't tell if a light is on.

"Let's go have breakfast. Sofie will be there, and we can ask her which room she's staying in," Catherine says.

I lose track of their conversation as they move away. At least, I hope they're moving away because I'm hungry and don't want to hide in my room all morning.

A few minutes later, I decide to make a move. Before I get the door open, someone else knocks on it. I stop in my tracks. The knocking continues. "Sofie, it's Judean. The coast is clear. Please let me in."

My breath catches as I quickly let her inside. She grabs the door from me and quickly closes it. "I'm sorry, but I'm hiding."

"Why?" I look her over. "Did you sleep elsewhere last night?" I grin, but it turns into a frown when I remember that Colton, the youngest Hawke brother, had led her away.

Judean's cheeks turn bright red, and I smirk as she closes her eyes and sighs. "I slept in his bed, but nothing happened. I woke up like this!" she hisses, holding her arms out to the side showing me the hockey jersey she wears. "How did I get into these clothes?"

"Well, did you ask Colton?" I sit in the chair at the dressing table, amused by my new friend's predicament.

"No, I didn't ask him! He was snoring when I snuck out."

Perching on the edge of the bed, she continues, "The blanket was pulled really low on his body. Like, below his firm butt. He's gorgeous and toned. I was so tempted to peek further, but I resisted."

"You slept next to a hot, naked guy and didn't peek?" I snort.

"Well, really? Look at me, then look at him." She slaps her thighs.

My brows pinch together. "I don't understand. You're both single and consenting adults, right? I mean, I think you are."

"I'm fat, so I'm single."

"Judean, who the hell put that notion into your head? I can't believe you'd say that about yourself. You have nice curves. You're pretty, and you have beautiful, glossy hair. I'm totally into guys, and even I've noticed your boobs. You're easy to be around and likable. You have so much going for you! And let's not forget that the guy slept naked beside you in his bed. That doesn't sound like someone who's not interested."

"I don't know. He's young."

I snicker. "How old are you?" I ask because she looks twenty.

"Twenty-four."

"Well, I think he's around your age."

"You're not helping. You're supposed to tell me what an idiot I am for running to you wearing one of his shirts."

"Judean, you're not an idiot. Maybe you should have stayed to see him while he was awake. You could be getting hot and sweaty with that man right now." I tug her up from the bed. "Change into something else so the others won't know about last night, because it's none of their business. Meet me in the restaurant for breakfast. I'm hungry."

"Okay! I can do that." She smiles and starts laughing. "I can't believe he tucked me into bed." She looks at me, then at the bed, then back at me. "Did you have company?"

"No."

"You can tell me. I promise I'm not spying on you for the others."

"He kissed me on the cheek and left me at the door. I promise." I sigh wistfully. "I would have broken my vows to Richard if Maddox had come inside with me."

"You're not married yet." She opens the door to my room, peers outside, and then walks out onto the porch. I walk in silence along the small pathways.

She's right. I'm not married yet. The sad truth is that I won't be marrying Richard Walker.

"I'll meet you shortly." Judean rushes off as soon as we step into the main building.

I follow the smell of food and find a cozy, delightful restaurant. It has a rustic feel and a sense of home. Warmth. I take a seat by the window, order a cup of coffee, and feel a sense of calm wash over me as I watch the world go by outside. The aroma of freshly baked bread fills the air, and I feel grateful for this unexpected moment of peace amidst the chaos. I do wonder where the others are.

Judean crashes into the seat opposite me. "Sorry." She winces. "The others are on their way, so I wanted to get here and warn you."

The server puts a cup of coffee down in front of Judean and shoots her a look I can't quite decipher. Judean and I exchange a glance, then watch the server stride away. "What was that about?"

"She got up on the wrong side of the bed," Judean says, taking a long drink. "It's a buffet-style breakfast, right?"

"Yes."

She pushes up from the chair. "Let's go. I could eat a horse."

"I'd planned on eating you, but you ran off," Colton says in a low, growly voice. He looks like he fell out of bed, threw on whatever he could find, and ran over here to find Judean.

"Are you calling me a horse?" Judean's spine stiffens as a frown appears on Colton's face.

"That's funny," Samantha says as she comes up behind us. I catch the server's attention for a few minutes before looking between Colton and Judean. Ah, that's why the server is grumpy. She has a crush on Colton.

Judean starts to tear up, and Colton curses loudly. "You are not a fucking horse!" he shouts, turning to Samantha, who has the good sense to back away. He calms down and says, "I'll let you eat breakfast." With that, he's gone.

I take Judean's elbow and lead her over to the food. "Just

breathe, okay? It was bad timing on Colton's part, but I was right. That man wants you." I shove a plate into her hands and take one for myself. "Food and a plan."

"What plan?"

"First, how I'm going to break off my engagement while I'm here and Richard is there. Second, how we're going to enjoy ourselves regardless of the others. Three, how you are going to apologize to Colton." I raise my brows.

"I can work on the first two. I'm not sure about the third." I let her grumble and mutter to herself while I fill her plate, doing the same for myself.

At least where I chose to sit is quiet, I think, but then I get sidetracked by Catherine.

"Can we speak for a moment, please, Sofie?"

Surprised by her soft tone, I nod. "Let me just put these down." I quickly mumble to Judean and head back to Catherine.

"I wanted to apologize for my behavior yesterday. The whole Alaska experience is out of the ordinary for me, and I took my irritation out on you. Can we please try to get along for the rest of the trip?"

"Sure," I say, surprising myself. "I'd like that."

"Good. After all, I'm going to be your mother-in-law." She smiles and sits at the table with the others, who have all listened in on our brief conversation. I'm also more than aware that her words weren't sincere.

Judean forces a blank expression when I sit down and admit. "I got an apology from Catherine. Every word she said was bullshit!" I smile feeling happy being here with my new friend.

"It's me and you, my friend."

Judean's eyes light as she raises a glass of orange juice. "To new friends and sexy men."

I snicker as we clink glasses.

Chapter Eleven

Maddox

WITH MY FEET UP ON THE SMALL COFFEE TABLE AND MY body comfortably nestled in a soft leather armchair, a hot cup of coffee in hand, this is the perfect way to enjoy the view from my back deck. I could spend hours here, listening to the bird's chirp and feeling the gentle breeze on my face. I imagine what it would be like to sit here with Sofie curled up on my lap. I sigh at my wishful thinking and take a slow sip of coffee.

"Bro, are you home?"

I sigh in annoyance, realizing that my peace has been disturbed by my youngest brother.

"You know women, right?" he asks, joining me.

I raise a brow, take a sip of coffee, and look at Colton, who looks perturbed. "Did Judean send your ass packing?"

"Not exactly, although she did leave before I woke up." He runs a hand through his hair and drops into another chair. "She said I called her a horse! Can you believe it? Making a lewd comment in front of Sofie might not have been the best idea, but I did not call her a horse!"

"It's too early in the morning for this." He grumbles, rubbing his eyes. "I haven't even had coffee yet. I saw that she had left, so I grabbed some clothes and ran after her."

"I see I'm not going to be rid of you until you spit it all out. Tell me why she got the wrong idea."

"She told Sofie that she was hungry and could eat a horse." He blushes and looks away. "I joked that I was going to eat her before she ran away." He winces. "It was the fucking truth. The woman is sexy as hell. I don't understand how she could have misinterpreted what I said."

I frown into my coffee, thinking over what he said. I don't see how the woman could have misunderstood him either. "You don't think she was embarrassed by your comment?"

"I don't know." He says quietly.

"Go get yourself a coffee." I nod toward the kitchen. "There are some croissants on the counter if you want one."

He pauses for a minute. "Thanks." He starts to move toward the kitchen, then stops. "Maddox?"

"Yeah?" I lift my gaze.

"I want to thank you for bringing me out here. I really

missed having my brothers around when you all abandoned Mom and me." He continues into the kitchen, and I watch him.

Is that how he felt when we moved to Alaska? Abandoned? I never thought of it like that. It wasn't like we all left together because we didn't. Hunter left first, and then we followed in our own time.

Coffee in hand, he adds, "I didn't mean anything when I said 'abandoned.' I guess that's how I felt, though. Mom too. But in the end, it worked out."

"Back to the present, then. Why don't you talk to Judean alone and apologize? Tell her that you want to take her on a date."

He winces. "I don't date."

I snort. "Then leave her alone. She's only here for four more nights anyway."

"So, you're just going to let Sofie leave?"

I reach up and rub the spot where my heart aches. "I won't ask her to stay. It must be her choice. I want her to be happy."

"At least she needs to know she has the choice." He salutes me as he leaves.

Peace. Again.

My hands sure like the feel of her.

My phone beeps.

After a stream of curse words leaves my mouth, I look at the screen.

Branson: Can you come by the
station ASAP?

I want to reply "no," but I don't. I drag my carcass out of the chair and take one long look outside at the valley beyond. Then, I close and lock the doors to the deck.

It takes no time at all before I pull up in front of the sheriff's station. Cursing at the sight of the crime scene unit's SUV parked one space over, I climb out of my truck and head inside. It's too early to deal with Janice.

Landon greets me with a tired nod. "He'll be glad you're here."

"Why? What's going on?" I ask, leaning on the counter between us.

He ignores the ringing phone—not the emergency line— and tells me, "Another body has been found."

"Fuck!" I run a hand through my hair and glance toward the hallway where my brother will be. "Is that why the crime scene unit is here?"

"Kind of." He winces. "The woman is annoying," he mutters under his breath. "I'd better answer the phone. They've been ringing all morning."

"Where's Sally?"

"She moved to Juneau with her boyfriend. No warning. Nothing." He pauses. "And before you ask, yes, I've confirmed that she's actually there. I spoke to her this morning."

"I'll go find the sheriff while you get the phone."

I trudge toward my brother's office, enter without knocking, and see that he's just hanging up the phone. The conversation stops, and Branson, Janice, and a guy I don't know turn to look at me. Branson finds his voice first. "Maddox, this is Janice's assistant, Roger Tyson."

Introduction over. "Why am I here?"

"You're here because we need help in the field," Janice says. "As you were at yesterday's scene, we figured you'd be the best person to help us today."

My eyes flicker to my brother, who looks extremely uncomfortable. He knows I hate seeing death. "Hunter is a sworn deputy. He should be here, not me."

I fold my arms and lean against the doorjamb. I'm not happy at all about this situation. Not just because of the dead body, but also because I know I'm only here because Janice decided she wanted me here. Instead of making a big deal about it, I say, "I've got things to do, so let's get started."

Janice follows me outside. I turn and say, "You need to stop this crap."

She takes a step back at the anger in my voice.

"Fucking hell!" I mutter. "I'm sorry. I have a busy day ahead, and this isn't helping, especially since it's not my job."

A horn blares, and I'm tempted to give my brother the finger. Instead, I shoot Garrett a glare. He's driving the minibus through town because he's leading a hike to the river and waterfall in the mountains. My gaze lands on Sofie as the bus passes by. Her eyes find mine before wandering to the woman beside me.

Well, shit.

"Was that Sofie Ryan?"

I snap my gaze to Janice. "How'd you know Sofie?"

"I don't know her. Her engagement pictures were in a magazine. She's marrying Richard Walker. His father owns half of San Francisco, not to mention a huge shipping company."

"How the hell do you know all this?"

"I just told you. A magazine. I never forget a face." She shrugs. "Would you like to ride with me? Branson can take Roger."

"No, I'll follow you." I climb into my truck, eager to get this over with. Now that I'm aware of what Sofie has to look forward to with Richard—a life of financial security in a big city—my mood has taken a nosedive. Then, of course, I wonder if she'll be happy.

What the hell is wrong with me? A day. Less than a day. A split second. That's all it took for me to fall for a woman who is out of my league. I slam my fist against the steering wheel while my brother bangs his fist against the window.

I drop the glass and wait, letting my irritation dissipate— at least outwardly.

"I'm struggling with this, Maddox," Branson admits, taking off his hat and running a hand through his hair. "It's weird as fuck, and it chills me to the bone. I wouldn't ask you for help if I didn't need it. You should know that by now." He pauses. "The body has gone." *Thank fuck!* "Hunter is out at the scene. It's too big of an area for us to cover without help."

"I'm an asshole," I mutter. "We're brothers. I'm always here to help. I've got a lot on my mind, is all."

He grunts and nods as he moves to his vehicle. That's when I notice the fire in Janice's eyes. Well, fuck me! This morning is going to be a barrel of laughs.

Chapter Twelve

Sofie

As we pass through town, I notice Maddox with an attractive blonde woman. I immediately wonder who she is and what their relationship is. I know I shouldn't be, but I find that I'm jealous. My stomach sinks at the thought of him with her. I shake myself and pay attention to Judean in the seat beside me.

For some reason that I haven't figured out yet, Richard's family are being nice today. My guard is still up around them, and that won't change. Something has changed since last night, and it's puzzling. They've been giving Judean the cold shoulder.

I don't really understand. Judean thinks it's because she's become my friend. I just hope things don't get any more complicated than they already are. Today's activities should give us enough space to take a breather and clear our minds. One can hope.

Garrett opens the door for us, and we step out into the fresh air of the forest. I smile widely as I close my eyes and breathe in the rich scent of pine trees. I'm excited for this walk-through Alaska's wilderness. We've all been given water and a packed lunch, which we'll eat at the river. Apart from Garrett, Ryland and Gabriel are with us, too.

I can't figure out the brothers. When we arrived at the lodge, I saw the way they looked at us and sensed that they were weighing their options. That's different today. They're all business, which I'm relieved about. The atmosphere is still tense, but at least they're not staring at us like we're fresh meat.

Ryland winks my way when I catch his eye. I chuckle and smile back, grateful for the moment of levity amidst the tension. Glancing around, I see that Judean looks rather pale as Samantha whispers to her. I frown. It can't be anything good because that woman never says anything nice.

I head toward them and clear my throat. "Ready, Judean?"

"Yeah." She breathes out a sigh of relief.

Samantha turns to face me with a fake smile. "We were just talking about dinner tonight." After giving Judean what I can only describe as a threatening glance, Samantha wanders over to her mother and the others. "She's full of shit!"

Judean snorts. "She wanted to know where your room is."

I huff out a frustrated breath. "Why do they want to know

that? Are they planning something? Ugh! I just want them to leave me alone. Let's enjoy ourselves and hope that Samantha and her mother face-plant into a pile of mud."

Judean gasps and snorts a loud laugh, drawing the others' attention. I nudge her. "Come on," I say.

"Ladies," Garrett says as he approaches us, his eyes drifting toward the others.

Judean and I turn and glance back at the group of women standing together, whispering and casting glances in our direction.

"Please let them find mud to slip in," Judean says under her breath.

Ryland chokes on a laugh and shakes his head.

I notice Gabriel, or Gabe as his brothers call him, standing back looking like he has the weight of the world on his shoulders. As we fall out, I take up the rear and fall in beside him. He glances my way and smiles. "Sofie," he says, his voice filled with warmth and sincerity. "You have my brother wrapped around your finger."

"Hmm," I mumble, unsure about that after seeing him with the blonde woman. "How are you doing? Maddox told me about Andrea. I'm sorry, Gabriel."

He blows out a breath. "I've been better, and it's Gabe." He winces. "I feel guilty," he says quietly. "If I had looked harder when she disappeared, maybe she would be alive today. I can't get that thought out of my head. She wanted to move in with me, but I didn't want her to. I didn't feel that way about her. I didn't care enough. Now she's dead."

I reach out and grip his arm, and we come to a stop. "Whatever happened has nothing to do with you, Gabe. You must know that. The only person responsible is the one who took her life. That wasn't you. It's not your fault that you didn't feel the same way about her. Tell me you know all this."

"I know that, yet it's easier said than done."

A loud whistle pierces the silence, and Gabe points toward the culprit—Ryland. "Move your asses."

"Ignore him," Gabe says as we move toward Ryland. "It's that time of the month," he adds as we pass him.

"Bro, not cool!"

I snicker. "The Hawke men are fun to be around." I glance at both men, who have dark eyes and facial scruff. "They're nice to look at, too," I add, moving to catch up with Judean.

"Did she just say we're hot?" Ryland says.

"No, she said you're mediocre and I'm hot," Gabe counters.

I shake my head at them and slide my arm through one of Judean's. "Are you doing, okay?"

"Being the butt of their jokes is getting old," she says sadly.

"We don't need them," I say quietly. "Besides, you have one of the delicious Hawke brothers after you. They don't!" I raise my eyebrows when she looks at me.

Her cheeks turn red. "He called me a horse."

"No, he didn't. He said he wanted to eat you for breakfast. You totally twisted his words around." I pat her hand. "I hear water in the distance." Pause. "Let me get my phone out. I want to take some pictures."

I take pictures of the tall trees with daylight peeking through and quickly point and click to capture an image of the two brothers. Ryland, catching sight of me, wraps an arm around his brother, and they both smile for the camera. I give them a thumbs-up in thanks and continue moving.

The leaves are vibrantly colored, and the sunlight filtering through them creates a beautiful contrast. As I continue my hike, I can't help but feel grateful for the opportunity to be here. Alaska in the summer is a beautiful, unforgettable experience.

An hour later, I trek through a small tunnel of trees and gasp in surprise. Before us, a river with crystal-clear water flows, and to the right, there is a gorgeous waterfall. It's breathtaking. The sound of the rushing water is soothing, and I pause to take in the beauty of the surrounding nature. I snap a few photos to capture the moment before moving up into the small clearing Garrett indicated.

We take off our backpacks and get out our water and lunch. I use my backpack as a seat, plopping down on it, glad for a rest and some refreshments. I chew on a chicken salad sandwich as I look through the photos I've taken. There aren't many, but the ones I took are good. Really good. I glance at the brothers and smirk when they each face me with a smile. I roll my eyes, but then I look away.

Judean groans beside me, so I glance her way, only to find that her eyes are elsewhere. I follow her gaze and see

Samantha heading our way. She stands in front of us for a moment before huffing out a breath and crouching down. "Why are you flirting with all the single men?" she asks.

I frown. "There's a difference between flirting and being friendly. I'm being friendly. They're nice guys." I shrug. "Actually, it's none of your business."

"It's Richard's business," she snaps. "He won't like it."

"Samantha, why don't you go back to your friends and enjoy this trip you planned instead of spying on me?"

"Hmph," she grunts, narrowing her eyes. She opens her mouth to give us both a tongue-lashing when shouting suddenly starts up. We glance in that direction and see Tisha batting away Ryland's hands, her screech sounds like a hyena's.

"What's that about?" Judean nudges me.

I shake my head. "I think he stopped her from falling into the water. Not that she seems happy about it."

"Stop touching me, you creep! Get away!" she shouts, struggling to push him away.

Catherine moves toward the group, and I decide to follow as does Judean.

"Get away from the edge!" Ryland snaps. "Unless you want to go for a swim downstream. Then I'll let you go like you keep asking me to."

Finally, Tisha shuts up and pushes Ryland away as she moves away from the edge of the four-foot drop into the river. She turns and points. "I'm going to report you to the sheriff for manhandling me."

Ryland huffs out a breath and mutters a curse about the

stupid woman under his breath. I don't blame him because she is stupid. Anyone could see that she was about to go for a swim.

"You are all witnesses!" Tisha continues.

"Now just a darn minute," Garrett begins.

I jump into the fray. "Tisha, the only thing I saw was Ryland stopping you from falling into the river. The current looks strong. You would have been pulled a good way downstream before anyone could reach you, and you wouldn't have been able to get yourself out. And that's if you didn't drown first! Frankly, I don't know what you're shouting about because you're the one who started this by going too close to the edge!" I pause for a second, then add, "Everyone here knows Ryland saved you. The question is, do they have the courage to be honest about it?" I move toward my backpack and put it on.

Gabriel clears his throat. "Everyone, pack away your trash and get into your packs. It's time to head back."

"The hot tubs await," Garrett says.

Judean winces.

"What?" I ask, helping her into her backpack.

"I hate being around people in my swimsuit."

I shrug. "Then don't wear one."

She gasps, then bursts into laughter.

Chapter Thirteen

Maddox

Hunter is standing by his truck, drinking water, so it takes him a few minutes to notice me walking toward him. Sweat coats my face. I wipe it away with the sleeve of my shirt. Too bad I can't do anything about the sweat in my groin. "I'd give my left nut for a shower right now," I say by way of greeting.

He grins. "You'd give both for one specific guest to be there with you." He drops the back of his truck and grabs me a bottle of water, which I accept gratefully. "I've got some protein bars in here if you want one or two."

I shake my head. "I just ate one. I forgot the water. I

should know better." Sighing, I glance back at where I came from, not relishing the idea of continuing. I will, though. Whoever this sick fuck is, he needs to be stopped.

"Bran thinks he already has another woman," Hunter says. "I've seen some messed-up shit, but what he's doing to these women is pure evil."

"Any tracks?"

"Not that I'm aware of." He huffs out a loud breath. "Honestly, bro, Janice is pissed at you, which means she's pissed at anyone called Hawke."

"She needs to get over herself." I retie my hair at the nape of my neck. "Can you imagine what she'd be like if I'd actually fucked her?"

"Wait!" He frowns. "You didn't—"

"No. I did take her out to dinner, but I soon realized she was extremely possessive. I lost interest the second I figured it out."

"She's hot."

"There are plenty more fish in the sea. Besides, do you really want to sleep with someone you work with?"

"I don't work with her," he says absentmindedly.

"Hunter!" Janice calls. "Can you come assist me?"

"What were you saying?" I chuckle as he moves away. Of course, I catch Janice glaring my way. I don't know what her problem is. I stare until Hunter reaches her, and her attention moves on.

My eyes wander over the other men and women taking a break from the search. The forest is huge and holds many secrets. I think back to when I found Andrea and wonder if she was the first. She left months ago, or so Gabe thought. Where has she been all this time? Has she been frozen since the moment she disappeared? I don't envy Branson right now.

He made the right choice when he appointed Hunter as a sworn deputy. He inherited Landon, and let's just say he needs a refresher course or ten. The man prefers the warmth of the office, which I can't blame him for in the winter months.

I toss my empty water bottle into the small recycling tub in the back of Hunter's truck before I take a few steps to meet Angie and Bud, the owners of Bud's bar. Angie has the brightest orange hair I've ever seen. She says she's never dyed it. They're both in their early sixties and plan to die behind the bar. Bud is a former Army Ranger with a never-ending stream of stories about his time in the service. They're both great people.

"This is going to be bad for business," Angie says.

I wince at her bluntness. "The news crews will arrive soon. They'll take all the available rooms and look for places to meet the locals." I raise an eyebrow and my lips twitch when Angie realizes that all isn't lost.

Bud grunts. "I can do without the vultures in my place."

"Our place." Angie glares at her husband, who smirks. "Our place, dear."

"Have you seen the sheriff?" Changing the subject is the only way to stop these two from bickering.

"I saw him with Hunter and that woman with a stick up her butt."

It's so unexpected that I burst out laughing, but then I catch myself because it's so damn inappropriate right now. "That would be the crime scene, boss."

"Yeah, well, she needs a good—"

Bud clamps a hand over Angie's mouth. Her eyes sparkle with mischief.

"No need to broadcast so loudly, Angie." I shake my head at the pair.

"We're heading back to open the bar early. There will be tea and coffee for anyone who wants to stop by," she says.

"That's good of you. I'll be sure to stop by."

"You're a good man, Maddox Hawke." Angie pats my arm and heads toward their truck. Bud hangs back and says, "If you need me and my rifle, let me know. Pass that along to your brother."

He holds my gaze until I nod.

I watch them drive off, then move toward Branson, who strides toward me with purpose. He's on a mission, and I have a feeling I'm not going to like what he has to say.

"A woman from the lodge called the station saying Ryland manhandled her. She wants to file a formal report with me," he hisses. "What the fuck is going on?"

"I'm here. With you. How the hell should I know?" I snap, taking a deep breath.

"Ask Sofie what happened before I go see the woman. Landon said she talked fast and that he thought her name was Trista."

"That name doesn't ring a bell... Tisha?"

"Right. Tisha." He yanks his hat off his head and runs a hand through his unruly hair. "Sorry, I snapped. I can do without that shit right now."

"Are we done here?" I nod toward the forest, where Janice and her crew are gradually reappearing and stepping into the parking lot.

"Yeah, I think so."

"I'll head back to the lodge." I pause. "Angie and Bud are offering free tea and coffee at the bar for anyone interested. I'll stop by briefly."

"I'll let everyone know." Branson turns and walks to meet Janice. She shoots me a long glare, and I feel her eyes on me as I pull away and head into town.

I make a quick stop at Bud's to show my face, then head to my cabin.

I'm in desperate need of a shower, so I decide to take one before I go find Sofie.

My damp hair is fastened up in what my mother insists is called a "man bun," and I'm dressed in my favorite color, black. I'm wearing a Henley shirt and jeans with my black biker boots. I'll be heading out on my Harley at some point. I step onto the porch of Sofie's cabin and hear giggling from inside. I pause for a moment, then realize I'm smiling to myself.

As I reach out to knock, the door flies open, and I'm

stunned. The toothpick in my mouth falls out as I gawk—there's no other word for it—at a nearly naked Sofie standing in front of me. I know Judean is standing beside her, but I can't tear my eyes away from all the skin Sofie is showing.

"Fuck me!" I vaguely hear Colton and sense him beside me, but my eyes are struggling to move.

Swallowing hard, I finally manage to look at Sofie's red face before my gaze drops to her fantastic breasts. Jesus! This woman was sent to test me. I'm sure of it. I swipe a hand down my face, but the image doesn't change. "What?" I croak, clearing my throat. "What are you wearing?"

"I was just about to ask Judean that." Colton stands beside me with his arms crossed over his chest, staring at the woman.

I shake my head and force my gaze to stay on Sofie's face. "What is that?" I wave my hand up and down between us, indicating her bikini.

Sofie rolls her eyes. "It's a bikini. We're going in the hot tub."

"They shortchanged you," I mutter, inhaling deeply. "Don't you have a cover-up or something?"

"Yeah, babe." Colton shoves in front of me. "Judean, you need to cover up that sexy fucking body. No one gets to see all your—" He waves a hand, indicating her chest. "All your—fucking hell—tits and ass," he hisses.

I notice the way Judean moves slightly behind Sofie, trying to hide from my brother's harsh words. I shove him to the side. "What he means is that he doesn't want another guy ogling you like he is."

"Damn right I don't!"

I hold Sofie's gaze. "I don't want anyone looking at you either."

"Oh, for goodness' sake! We're going into the hot tub with the others. There won't be any men in them with us. Stop acting like Netherlanders." Sofie shakes the material she had been holding and slips it over her head. Judean does the same. "Happy now?" She grabs Judean by the elbow and tugs her forward. "We'll get going."

They step around us. It takes a few moments to realize that I haven't asked Sofie about Ryland and Tisha. "Wait up! I need to borrow Sofie for a moment." I take my woman and walk her back inside the cabin while Colton takes her place beside Judean.

"Maddox, what's gotten into—"

My mouth finds hers the second the door shuts behind us. I grab her butt, hoisting her up against the door, and move in to press my body against hers. Our tongues slide together as the kiss deepens into languid strokes. I shudder when her fingers slide through my hair. Her pussy rubs frantically against my hard dick while Sofie moans into my mouth. I didn't bring her in here for this. I've lost my mind. For her. This is nuts.

I use my body to keep her pressed against the door and tug on the string holding her tiny panties together. Her mound is perfect, lightly dusted with hair. Her breasts heave as I hold her gaze and slip a finger between her legs. Her body quivers, and when I feel how wet she is for me, I nearly lose it completely. The moment I slip my finger inside her warm, wet pussy, she falls apart. Her back arches, thrusting her breasts into my face. Her head slams against the door behind her. I descend on her breasts, biting down on a hard nipple. Her fingers dig into my shoulders. She lets out a loud, keening wail, and her body pulses around my digit as she comes.

My dick is so hard that I don't know how I've managed to stave off my orgasm. I want to shove my jeans down and pin her to the door with my cock. I'd come just from being inside her. That's how wound up I am right now.

"Oh," she whispers once she's come back down to earth.

I drop my forehead to hers, panting harshly, and grin. "You're fucking beautiful when you come." Her cheeks are red, and her lips are swollen, which causes my heart to clench.

"We shouldn't have done this."

My heart falls to my feet.

Her fingers dig into my arms. "I mean, I haven't told Richard that I can't marry him yet." She pants. "I've removed the ring."

Delighted to hear that, I turn and carry her to the bed, being careful not to crush her as I follow her down. I surround her and brush my lips over hers. "You need to tell him." I whisper, feeling a rush of excitement when one of her leg's curls around my hips.

"I will." She places her hands on my face, using her fingers to brush my hair behind my ears. With her hands still on my face, she looks deep into my eyes and says, "I need that part of my life to be over."

My heart pounds against my breastbone, and I close my eyes in relief. Opening them again, I notice a soft smile on Sofie's lips. I lean down and kiss her before climbing off her. Wincing, I adjust myself and offer her a gentle smile. I offer her my hand and help her off the bed. I retrieve her cover-up and panties.

"You do know there are only going to be women in the hot tub, right?" She says struggling to fasten the strings of her bikini panties.

I gather one side and fasten it for her while she does the other. Then, I take the cover-up and slip it over her head, exhaling when she's covered. "My brothers have perfect vision, Sofie. I trust them around you, but I don't want them seeing you half-naked." I shrug. "I'm a possessive asshole."

Suddenly, she wraps herself around me. "I like the possessive asshole in you." She moves away and pokes me in the belly. "I'd better go rescue Judean." She snickers. "Your brother has a thing for her, huh?"

"My baby brother needs to keep it in his pants with the guests."

She raises an eyebrow. "Really?"

"He's twenty-three. He plays the field. Your friend is too nice for Colton to fuck and then walk away, which he will do."

"Oh."

I run my hands through my hair and offer a wry grin. "I was coming to get the story about Ryland and Tisha." Her eyes shoot up, so I continue, "She's filed an official complaint with the sheriff's office."

Gasping, Sofie gives me a startled look. "I can't believe she did that." Pause. "Actually, I can." Puffing out a breath, she stands with her hands on her hips. "Tisha was trying to take a picture and stood too close to the edge. Ryland pulled her back. She said he touched her without permission. From the looks of things, she would have fallen into the river if he hadn't grabbed her. I didn't see it all go down. I heard about it." She winces. "I'll talk to her."

"I'm not sure that's such a good idea. She'll want to know how you know." I shrug. "Let's get you and Judean into the hot tub." I wrap an arm around her shoulders, give her a brief hug, and open the door.

Chapter Fourteen

Sofie

As Maddox ushers me out the door, I can still feel his touch on my skin. I meet Judean's flushed gaze, then look at Colton, who looks disgruntled. I hide my snicker behind a pleasant grin. "Judean, are you ready to get wet?"

Her eyes widen. Maddox huffs, trying not to laugh. Colton smiles as widely as he can.

"Oh my God! Get your minds out of the gutter!" I move forward and grab Judean by the elbow. As I move past Colton, I shoot him a glare. He snaps his mouth closed, but his eyes dance with mischief. "Keep walking," I whisper to Judean.

As we approach the end of the path, we see the others are

already in the hot tub. I look back at Colton and Maddox, who are standing together with their arms crossed and grinning mischievously at us. I can't help but laugh as we reach the deck.

It's difficult to choose which hot tub to get into because Catherine is in one and Samantha in the other. I decide to go for Samantha's, as there is room for the two of us. I shake off my cover-up, step into the water, and sit down, sighing. "Whoever made the decision to do this, thank you!"

"That would be me," Samantha says.

"The water is delightful and just what I need." Of course, my mind wanders to Maddox, and I wonder what it would feel like to be in here alone with him. My skin tingles at the thought—not to mention, my nipples throb into hard buds.

Hearing disgruntled muttering, I open my eyes and see Samantha looking at Judean as she climbs into the tub.

"Judean, what are you wearing? You have too much weight to carry that off. It's not flattering on you at all."

Judean pauses with one leg in the tub. My brows must have shot up into my hairline at the cold, harsh words. I've never known anyone to be so hateful to another person.

"What the hell?" I finally hiss. "There's nothing wrong with Judean." I stand as Judean pulls away from the tub. "I can't say the same about you!" I snap at Richard's sister.

I shiver on the deck, but I ignore it as I hurry to put my flip-flops on and grab the cover-up. I set off the way Judean bolted. I'm furious at Samantha's cold-heartedness. What the hell is her problem? Her mother is just as cold and evil. Why didn't I ever stand up for myself back home? Ugh! I know why. Being out here in this beautiful place and meeting Maddox has truly opened my eyes. I've changed in the short time I've been here. The fact that I'm relieved not to be here with Richard says it all.

I slow down and realize that I have no idea where Judean ran off to. Once my heart slows, I hear sniffles. They're coming from the path that leads to the family cabins. I quickly move in that direction and find Judean sniffling into Maddox's chest. A quick wave of jealousy hits me, but I shake it off. There's no reason for that here. He spots me and his eyes plead for help while cooing to an upset Judean.

I place a gentle hand on Judean's back. "Judean, she's a bitch. Please don't believe what she said."

She lifts her tear-stained face, and I find myself pulled into her and Maddox. "I've never had a threesome before," I joke, trying to lighten the mood.

Maddox catches my gaze and raises an eyebrow. I smirk and shake my head. My attention turns to Judean, who chuckles. "She's jealous of you. You have gorgeous curves, while she's stick thin with a horrible personality." I waggle my brows. "And let's not forget how the very sexy Colton Hawke is trying to get into your pants."

"Oh my God," Judean says, hiding her face in her hands and laughing.

Maddox glares. "You called my brother sexy!"

I roll my eyes. "You Hawke men are gorgeous, so get over

yourself." I pat him on the chest. "You're the only one I imagine naked, if that makes you feel better."

"Can you not dirty talk your man while I'm within earshot?" Judean sighs and lets out a loud puff of air. "I always let her get to me. I was really looking forward to a soak."

"I have a hot tub on the back deck that you can both use."

We turn to look at Maddox. My face lights up with excitement. "Are you sure you don't mind?"

"You could join us, too," Judean suggests.

My face heats as I remember my recent thoughts about Maddox and me in a hot tub.

He catches my gaze. "I'm not sure that's a good idea." He chuckles, captures my hand, and then grabs hold of Judean's. He leads us through the kissing trees and out to the area where the family cabins are. I glance at Judean, who looks delighted at the sight. Maddox clears his throat and says, "In case you're wondering, Colton lives in the cabin with the yellow Yamaha parked outside. He rides in the forests and on dirt tracks."

"Is that so?" I say, though Judean stays silent, her eyes linger in that direction. I nudge her and smirk. She rolls her red, swollen eyes.

There was no need for Samantha to treat Judean the way she did. The more I think about it, the more I wonder if what I said is true—that Samantha is jealous of Judean. I mean, my friend has a great body, with dips and curves. I'd love to have her breasts for starters.

Inside Maddox's home, he squeezes my hand before

releasing me and striding toward the glass doors leading to the deck. He slides them open. "Here you go, ladies. Total privacy with an awesome view." He looks out toward the mountains while I take in his towering form. My heart kicks into overdrive at the sight of this delicious man. "I agree," I say huskily, meeting his gaze. "The view is awesome." I smile as a slight blush coats his cheekbones. That's a surprise.

Judean clears her throat. "Is it okay to get in?"

"It is." Ever the gentleman, he holds out his hand to help Judean climb in. Turning to me, his eyes darken as they rove over my bikini-clad body. He doesn't offer me his hand. Instead, he wraps an arm around my waist and clamps a hand on my hip.

By the time I get into the hot tub, I'm sure my face is as hot as my body. I avoid Judean's knowing look and turn to Maddox. "Thank you for this. It's kind of you."

He snorts. "What guy wouldn't want two hot women in his hot tub?"

"Hot women!" Colton shouts.

My gaze shoots to Judean, who frantically tries to hide her face.

"Bro, are you holding out on me?" Colton appears in the doorway. Maddox puts a hand on Colton's chest to keep him from coming out to the deck.

"Don't you ever knock?" Maddox grouches.

"Not when I see my woman heading in here. No, I don't fucking knock." He shoves Maddox's hand away and strides toward us. He stops in his tracks when he sees Judean's tear-stained face. "Why have you been crying?"

"Colton!" Maddox hisses. "There's something called tact."

"She's been crying. Why?"

I watch the younger Hawke brother, noting how every part of his body is coiled to attack, anger seething from every pore. Every inch of him tells me that he has a serious thing for Judean. I thought so but seeing him this way after she cries confirms it.

"One of the other guests made some horrible comments," I say.

"What would you like to drink? Tea? Coffee? Water? Beer?" Maddox asks, redirecting the conversation.

"What other guest?" Colton stands with his arms crossed and his legs slightly spread. I must admit, he looks good in black pants and a white shirt. His name tag, which is attached to the breast pocket, tells me that he's about to start work because I didn't see him thirty minutes ago in the lobby.

"Coffee would be nice," I say.

"For me as well. Thanks, Maddox." Judean smiles, and I notice Colton's frown deepen.

These brothers are intense.

Maddox grabs his brother's arm and moves him inside. I finally let out a breath and look at Judean. I can't help but smile and giggle a little. I smother it behind a hand.

"I need a cold shower after that," Judean sighs. "Something tells me not to let Colton know who upset me."

I snicker. "I totally agree with that."

The water is lovely and warm, and I feel the tension slowly melting away. Judean sighs and rests her head back against the side of the tub. I lean back as well, but I stare out at the view. "Peace and quiet," I think, just as I hear more than two male voices from inside. Judean glances at me, startled, but I shake my head. "There are eight of them, plus a silver fox of a dad, so just enjoy the view."

"Hey, bro, did you know you have two babes in the hot tub? Sophie called Dad a silver fox." Spencer shouts, and I inwardly groan, feeling my cheeks heat.

"I like being called a babe," Judean whispers.

Chapter Fifteen

Maddox

Dad blushes after Spencer announced what he overheard. I shoot him a look and he stops teasing as I take the two coffees out to Sofie and Judean. I kiss Sofie's head as I head back inside. I close the door, leaving a small gap so I can hear if they need me. "Give them some alone time," I tell Spencer.

I feel his eyes on me as I move into the kitchen and start making a large pot of coffee. I know that if three of my brothers are here, the others will follow. Well, maybe not Branson. He's going to be working around the clock. Dad's here, too. I know he was tickled hearing what the girls called him. I just hope it doesn't go to his head like it would my brothers'.

I shoot Colton a sideways glance. He continues to sit quietly, stewing about Judean. He isn't stupid, so I'm sure he's figured out that one of their group upset Judean. That whole family needs a wake-up call. I may be a jerk sometimes, but I don't go around putting people down. That isn't okay.

My brother catches my eye, and his eyes narrow. "I bet it was Samantha, wasn't it?"

"What did Samantha do?" Garrett asks.

I sigh heavily and lean on the countertop. "Yes, it was Samantha. She said some hurtful things to Judean." I shrug. "I invited them here to use my hot tub. I promised they wouldn't be disturbed."

"Tell me what she said!" Colton stands, his body rigid with anger.

"I don't know exactly what she said, but from what I overheard, it had something to do with her figure." I wince.

"There's nothing wrong with her!" Colton hisses. "She makes me hard as a rock."

Dad chokes on his coffee. "Son—"

"It's true! Jeez, Dad. You have eight sons. You know what I'm talking about." Colton's eyes pop wide as Hunter and I gawk at him. "You know what? I sure as hell don't want to think about you and Mom getting it on." He shudders. "I can't believe I went there." Tossing a wave over his shoulder, he leaves.

"What did I hear about Tisha reporting Ryland?" Garrett asks.

"I'll be glad to see the back of those women," Dad says. "They have no right to come here and cause problems over stupid things."

"Three nights left," I say, my eyes drifting toward the back deck. I wonder if I'll get to keep Sofie here in Hawke's Ridge.

"Don't worry, son," Dad says, putting a hand on my shoulder. "We'll all make sure she has no option but to stay."

I roll my eyes and stare at Dad's back as he walks into the living room. I sigh and turn to Garrett. "She reported Ryland to Branson because he grabbed her to keep her from falling into the river."

"That's messed up!" He glances at the door Colton left through and nods. "What's gotten into the little *puck?*"

I snort. "The *puck* has a thing for Judean." I grin, amused by Garrett's nickname for the youngest family member. At twenty-three, Colton is trying to sleep with every guest at the lodge—he's almost succeeded. At least he has the sense not to bring anyone home. "Puck" is the more polite word, after all. Mom would be furious if she heard Garrett calling her baby a little fuck.

Branson stomps inside, glancing around the room before his eyes land on me. I inwardly groan, wondering what that look is all about. It can't be good.

"Hello, son. I hope you're eating. Your mother won't be happy if you're not taking care of yourself."

"Dad, I'm fine. Busy. But yes, I am eating."

Dad nods as Branson removes his jacket. He takes off his hat and runs his fingers through his hair before joining Garrett and me in the kitchen. I shove a steaming mug of coffee in front of him and pull-out bread, cheese, mushrooms, tomatoes, and hot sauce. Grilled cheese is quick and our favorite snack.

Neither of my brothers says anything until I put everything on the grill. "So," I say, leaning against the countertop, "tell us what's happening."

"I've pissed Janice off," Branson hisses. "The woman has some issues." He shakes his head. "She was holding out on information until I got you down there to take her out to dinner. I was furious. I went into my office to get away from her, and just then, her boss called. I let him have it about her. I've had enough. He was shocked and said he would resolve the situation. He's sending a new guy to take her place."

He sighs. "Like a fucking pussy, I snuck out the back and came up here. She's crazy, so I'm relieved you're not dating her."

Garrett snickers. "You're the sheriff, and you're hiding from one little woman."

He snorts. "You wouldn't laugh at me so quickly if you'd met her." He glances toward the back deck, and his eyes widen. "Why are there two naked women on your back deck?" His eyes haven't moved as he leans over for a better look.

"Bro, lean any farther and you'll be on the floor," Garrett chuckles.

"Explain!" Branson narrows his gaze at me and nods toward the deck.

"I'm sick of repeating it. Just stop ogling Sofie. She's mine. Judean is free and single."

Garrett coughs. "Are we sure about that? Because the little puck has a hard-on for her."

Branson winces. "Colton and 'hard-on' should not be in the same sentence."

I laugh, plate the sandwiches, and grab the ones for the girls. Garrett will fill you in about the trouble the others in the party are causing. Oh, and Tisha. She was about to fall into the river when Ryland grabbed her and stopped her from being swept downstream."

"Fucking hell! Dealing with crazy women is not how I want to end my day." He pauses and runs a hand down his face. "Sally just left me in the lurch."

Garrett and I stare at him. I'm sure my brother is trying to figure out who Sally is. Exasperated with him, Branson curses. "My assistant!"

"You mean the one who decides what hours she's working on a particular day? That assistant?" asks Garrett.

Branson looks pissed. "Yeah."

"Landon mentioned her earlier. Did you speak to her? I'm not sure I'd take Landon's word for it."

"Unfortunately, I have. Apparently, she's had enough of doing Landon's job for him. She's found a better job with the same pay and fewer responsibilities. She told me to go fuck myself." His brows drew together. "I'm not a jerk of a boss, am I?"

Remembering the sandwiches in my hands, I say, "Give me a minute to drop this off outside." I step out onto the back deck and tell myself not to imagine myself naked in the hot tub with an equally naked Sofie. Yeah, I need to stop thinking about that.

Hearing Judean giggle pulls me out of my lustful thoughts, and I grin. "I thought you ladies might be hungry."

"Oh, he cooks as well," Sofie teases, her face alight with mischief. "Do you have a couple of towels we can use?" she asks as she stands. I nearly swallow my tongue when the water falls away and I get a look at her body. I can't speak. The lush swell of her breasts is barely contained behind the two triangles, which have become transparent. Her plump nipples and areoles have my dick hard as a fucking spike.

I move my gaze lower and quickly snap it up to her flushed face. "Sit back down," I say, blowing out a breath. "Do not stand up until I'm back with towels."

I race inside and grab two extra-large bath towels. Nothing smaller will do. On my way through the house, I stop. Dad, Branson, and Garrett have disappeared. Then, I hear chuckling from outside.

"Fuck!" I narrow my eyes on Garrett as I stalk toward him. His eyes light up. "What are you doing out here?"

Branson chuckles and wraps an arm around my shoulders. "Did you just laugh?" I ask.

"You're imagining it," he says dryly.

"Pfft! Imagining my ass!" I shake him off and glare at my brothers. "Turn around while they get out of the tub."

Sofie looks amused as I step to the edge of the tub and fluff out a towel. "I won't peek." Regardless of how much I want to get another look at the gorgeous woman, I snap my eyes closed.

She snickers. "You've already seen me, Maddox." I open my eyes just in time to see the water sluicing down her body once more. Her bikini is just as transparent as before.

I clear my throat, catch her under the arms with the towel, and lift her out. I wrap the towel around her. I wink at Judean. "Your turn." The woman blushes furiously, but I don't give her time to refuse. "Let's have you."

She stands and stops me from lifting her. "I'm too heavy," she whispers, looking down.

"Damn that woman," I mutter under my breath. "Look at me, Judean." She tentatively lifts her gaze. "There's nothing wrong with you. Now, I'm going to help you like I did Sofie if that's okay?"

She nods after a moment.

I help her out of the hot tub, and once both women are on the deck wearing cover-ups over their towels, we sit around the outdoor table with my dad and two brothers. Branson keeps looking at his phone, then sighs and ignores it. Seeing me watching, he sighs again.

"I need a new assistant," he grumbles.

"You also need to send Landon to Anchorage for training. He's a liability right now," I add.

"Assistant?" Judean asks, tilting her head toward my brother. "What kind of assistant?"

Sofie frowns at her friend.

Chapter Sixteen

Sofie

BRANSON LOOKS AT JUDEAN AND SAYS, "IT'S MORE OF AN office manager position. I need someone to answer the phones, use the mainstream computer database, and to handle general administrative duties."

Judean nods, a thoughtful expression spreading across her face. Then she smiles. "I work as a clerk for the San Francisco Police Department." Her grin widens as Branson raises his eyebrows. "I'd love to try it out while I'm here. If we get along, I'd expect a formal offer. How does that sound?"

"Answer to his prayers," Garrett says, patting his brother

on the shoulder. "And to Colton's," he adds quietly. I glance his way, and he winks.

I roll my eyes and smirk as I look back at Judean, who looks excited. "Are you sure about this?"

"More than I've ever been sure about anything in my life." She grins, her eyes lighting up with excitement. "I can do the job Branson needs me to do. I've been doing it for two years." For Branson. "I have a degree in business and criminology. I can do this!"

Branson sighs. "This is your vacation, though."

She shakes her head. "Being told I'm fat and that I look ridiculous is not my idea of a vacation. I'm all yours. What time should I report tomorrow?"

Momentarily stunned, Branson frowns. "Is eight, okay?"

"I'll be there."

"I live in a cabin here. I'll pick you up out front of the lodge at eight."

"Now that's settled," Maddox says. "Do you have any dinner plans?" His eyes flicker between Judean and me before settling on my face. My heart flutters. I'm glad I'm wearing a thick towel, so he can't see my reaction to him.

Judean nudges me, and I snap out of it. "Dinner?"

"We don't have plans."

"Well, we're supposed to have dinner with everyone tonight," Judean says.

I groan because I hate that I'm going to disappoint Maddox. "I guess we're going to have to be good and eat with them." I smile. "But afterwards, we could get dessert together."

Maddox, Garrett, and their father, all stare at Branson, who flushes and rolls his eyes. "Okay, I can whip up dessert for everyone." He looks at his family. "You all have to eat elsewhere," he says.

"As long as we get dessert, I'm good with that." Maddox turns to Judean and me. "If Branson ever decides to quit being a cop, he could make it as a chef."

"Not really, but I can make a mean dessert." His lips twitch. "I need to go and sort something out." He stands. "Catch you later." He heads out, leaving me with an uneasy sensation in the pit of my stomach. Maddox told me that he's working a dangerous case, and now Judean is going to be right there with him.

A shiver brushes over my neck and shoulders as I stand. "I'm going to head out as well." Judean gets to her feet. "I need a shower and some clothes," I add. "Thank you for everything."

"I'll walk with you," Maddox says as he gets to his feet. He adds to his dad and brother, "Show yourselves out."

"I really like your family." I sigh, softly.

"I'm going to let you two catch up alone." Judean moves around the table, but Maddox gently grabs her arm.

"I'll walk you both back." He smirks. "Or would you prefer I ask Colton to do that?" He raises his eyebrows.

I nudge him, chuckling. "Stop teasing her."

"Hey, my brother whom Garrett calls 'the puck' has a real crush on you, Judean."

"Pfft," Judean scoffs. "The *puck* will be hounding someone else tomorrow," she snickers. "The *puck!*"

I chuckle, but wisely keep my mouth shut, as does Maddox.

In the garden, Judean heads off to her room, insisting that she can find it alone. She winks at me and nods toward Maddox. Not one part of that was subtle.

"I'm not going to come inside with you," he says, his brows pull together. "I don't suppose you want to move to Alaska?"

I stare at the man, surprised, as he looks at me with one brow raised. His features are sharp, and he has beautiful lips and gorgeous eyes. "I take it that's a no." He takes my elbow and moves us along while I finally find my voice.

"I'm not saying no. It hasn't occurred to me before that it might be an option." I pause on the steps leading to my cabin. "I have some decisions to make, which means I'll have to head back to Frisco in a few days." I feel my shoulders sag, because I want to tell this man—whom I hardly know—that yes, I will stay and work here in Hawke's Ridge. "I took time off work for this trip. I already have vacation time booked for the wedding." I smile. "I'd like to spend that time here with you."

"Thank fuck for that." He pulls me into a hug, and I melt against him. I wrap my arms around his broad shoulders and rub the back of his neck with my fingers. A soft growl rumbles out of him, and I feel his arousal pulsing against my belly. "You better go inside."

I squeeze him tightly, then let go—but not before quickly brushing my lips over his. "I'll see you later for dessert."

"I'll pick you and Judean up from the restaurant at 9:30, if that works for you."

"Perfect."

I watch the beautiful man stride away, enjoying the way his ass sways in the black jeans he's wearing. He glances back over his shoulder and smirks when our eyes meet. He knows exactly where I was looking.

Shaking my head, I step inside the cabin and come to a complete stop.

My blood freezes and I stare. My anger builds with each breath until I finally force out, "What are you doing here?"

"I thought I'd surprise you," Richard says, moving into my personal space and kissing my cheek. "You look surprised."

Snapping out of it, I say, "Of course I'm surprised!" I move away from him and notice his suitcase. I point. "You are not staying in this cabin with me."

"Sofie, stop being difficult. I'm your fiancé." He smiles as though everything is perfect. I narrow my eyes. "Spit it out, Richard," I snap. "I know either your mother or sister called you."

"They have nothing to do with me being here."

"You don't do anything without your mother knowing." I hiss. Grabbing his case, I wheel it toward the door until he steps in my way. "Move."

"Mother was right! You've changed in the few days you've been here." Richard takes his case and moves it further into the room.

Frustrated and angry, I head into the wardrobe, unlock the safe, and retrieve my engagement ring. I take a deep breath and exhale slowly to calm my nerves. I turn and thrust the ring at Richard. "I'm really sorry. I didn't want to do it like this, but I can't marry you. You're a nice guy, but you need someone who gets along with your family. Someone who loves you." I wince. "I'm really sorry."

He stares at the ring, then at me, but doesn't make a move to take it, so I quickly tuck it into the pocket of his jacket. I chance a glance and he looks furious. It's the first time I've seen him become so angry. Nerves start in my belly as I slowly step away from him.

"I'll call the front desk and have them find you a room because you're not staying with me."

"What's going on, Sofie?" He sits on the edge of the bed. "Don't I deserve more than this?" He waves his hands around before they form into fists. Surely, he's not going to hit me. A rush of fear hits me followed by a wave of guilt. "You deserve more, and I realize I can't give you that." Pause. "I deserve more, too, Richard. What I'm feeling isn't new. I've felt out of sorts, as if the wedding is rushing ahead and I'm not ready. I really am sorry."

"Were you going to tell me in person or over the phone that the wedding is off?"

"I planned on telling you when I got home. I didn't know you were already on your way here."

He nods. "There are no rooms available. A busload of guests checked in ahead of me. They got the last rooms. It's a large bed. There's no reason why we can't share."

No, no, no.

"That can't happen."

Richard mutters under his breath. "You're being ridiculous."

"Your mother brought you here, so share with her!" I snap. "Please leave."

"Why are you angry with me? I haven't asked you about the guy you've been seen with. If anything, I should be angry."

I huff and rub a hand across my brow. "Why aren't you angry with me?"

"Because I know this is cold feet about the wedding. That's all it is. Mother said so. Samantha, too. That's why I'm here. I'm here to remind you that I love you. You'll come around." He gets to his feet and starts moving with the suitcase into the dressing room.

"Fuckity fiddlesticks!" I mutter, wondering what the hell I'm going to do.

I pick up my phone and quickly message Judean.

Chapter Seventeen

Maddox

After showering, I put on dark gray slacks and a white button-down shirt and quickly glance at myself in the mirror. I don't usually pay much attention to how I look, but it's nice to clean up and dress nicely occasionally. Am I going through too much trouble for dessert, though? I splash on cologne and realize I'm not doing this for dessert. I'm doing it for Sofie. I want her to know she's worth the effort.

My phone starts ringing and vibrating on the dressing table. I wince when I see Branson's name on the screen. I hesitate for a moment, debating whether to answer. In the end, I answer because I saw Hunter head into his cabin not too long ago, which means Branson must be out there with minimal backup. "Everything okay?"

He sighs. "No, it isn't. Can you come?"

I close my eyes and silently curse. "Where?"

"My office. A couple of feds are here." He hangs up, and I stare at my phone.

"Fucking hell!" I shove my feet into boots instead of shoes and head into the living room. I quickly send Garrett a message, asking him to meet Sofie and Judean, and then I head out via the main lodge. I need to see Sofie.

I spot the group of women sitting around a large, circular table. The other group of tourists who checked in earlier are spread throughout the room. Yet, my eyes land on Sofie, but they quickly flicker to the guy sitting with her.

Sofie notices me and quickly rushes over before I can step toward her. She takes my arm and leads me out of the room. "He showed up. I can't get rid of him."

"Your fiancé?" I frown.

"My former fiancé. I gave him his ring back, but he insists that I only have cold feet. I don't. I've told him this. He was in my cabin when you walked me back. He won't leave. There are no rooms."

"Wait, he's staying with you?" My mouth tightens as I take a step away from Sofie. I don't want the woman I'm falling for to sleep with someone else, even if he is—or rather, was—her fiancé.

Sofie steps with me and grabs my face. "I'm not in the mood to be misunderstood, so I'll spell it out for you. I'm not engaged anymore. Richard thinks we are. But he has the ring. I won't wear it ever again. I don't want him in my room, but he won't leave."

"You can stay with me."

"What?"

I shrug. "I want you with me, so it makes sense that you stay with me. I sure don't want you anywhere near another man."

Her lips twitch. "Are you jealous, Maddox Hawke?"

"Damn straight I am." I grab her hips and pull her up against me. My mouth crashes against hers, hard and needy. My tongue joins in, and the moment she sucks hard, my cock tries to punch out of my pants. Breathing heavily, I gently push her away. "I want you to move into my cabin, okay? I'll ask Garrett to stop by your cabin and help you gather your things before taking you out for dessert." Pause. "I should be back soon, but I'm not sure. Branson has a situation down at the station. I need to go back him up." I pause when it hits me. "Wait, dessert is going to be delayed. Possibly a raincheck. I'll let you know."

"Forget about dessert. You won't be in danger, will you?"

"The feds are in town," I whisper, kissing the tip of her nose. "Keep that to yourself."

"I will. Be careful."

I pull her close and wrap my arms around her, breathing in the citrus scent of her hair. "I have you to come home to."

"Mmm."

I hate leaving her right now, but I have no choice. "I need to go. Will you be, okay?" I nod toward the dining room.

"I'll be fine."

I kiss her forehead and rush out the front door, shooting another message to Garrett.

As I PULL UP OUTSIDE THE SHERIFF'S STATION, I NOTICE THE large black SUV parked next to the equally large sheriff's utility vehicle. They got here quickly. I step inside the station and move toward Branson's office. His eyes widen when he notices me. Considering what I'm wearing, I'm not surprised. He grimaces as I step into his office. "Sorry, I interrupted your evening." He waves a hand toward the two Feds. A woman and a man. "Agents Sheridan and Kalluk. This is my brother, Maddox."

I nod, slightly confused as to why I'm here. I have no law enforcement experience, and I only help Branson out occasionally. "How are you here in town?" I finally ask, breaking the silence, because my brother looks ready to explode.

The woman turns to me and holds out her hand. "Agent Adele Sheridan." I shake her hand, and she continues. "We've been tracking a predator. When the sheriff started a search with certain parameters, an alert was sent to my phone. Our brief research mentions that one of your brothers, Gabriel Hawke, was the last person to see the victim, Angela Stevens." She pauses. "Gabriel Hawke was also in Montana when three women were killed. The crime scenes were identical as the one you just discovered."

My blood runs cold at what the agent is suggesting. I realize this is why I'm here when I meet Branson's furious yet tired gaze. "You're wasting time going after Gabe. He wouldn't harm a fly," I defend.

"Then how do you explain his whereabouts? He has been at each location."

I frown at the young agent and wonder why the older one is letting her take the lead. I give her my attention and ask, "If you think our brother is the killer, why are you telling us?"

"Because," Kalluk states, "Agent Sheridan doesn't believe your brother *is* the killer." He sighs. "I've learned to trust her instincts."

I shoot my gaze her way and notice a blush coating her cheekbones.

"Please explain?"

"I have a very good built-in psychopath antenna. He doesn't register at all. I honestly believe he's a genuinely nice guy."

"You've met him?"

She winces. "I sat next to him at a bar in Anchorage." She shrugs. "What I do believe is that the killer might be following your brother. I think he's someone Gabriel Hawke knows, or at least someone he's met in passing."

"You're talking about a stalker, right?" Branson asks, rubbing the stubble on his chin as he sits sprawled out in his chair. I don't miss the quick look Sheridan gives him before getting back to business. I hide my amusement because now isn't the time.

"A stalker, maybe. We don't know anything else."

"In fact, we don't have evidence to prove your brother isn't the killer, just like we can't prove he is," Kalluk adds. "All we have so far are his whereabouts over the past six months."

"Fuck," I curse. "You need to speak to Gabe in the morning. Not here, but at the lodge." I keep my gaze on Branson.

He nods. "Meet me at the front of the lodge at 7:30, and I'll walk you to his cabin. He'll answer your questions. He didn't do this."

"Afterwards, I want to see where the bodies were found," says Sheridan.

"That can be arranged. I have a new assistant starting tomorrow, so I must get her settled first thing, but I can show you around after that."

"That suits." Kalluk stands and offers me his hand. We shake hands, and before releasing me, he says, "My nephew speaks highly of you, Maddox Hawke. I hope we find your brother innocent." Releasing my hand, he turns to Branson. "Sheriff."

Nephew. I rack my brain for a name, but none comes to mind. "How do I know your nephew?"

"You rescued him from a burning car when he was trapped inside."

My eyes widen in surprise. "Jonny Nanuq," I say quietly.

He nods. "He values your friendship."

"I value his too. He's a good man." I smile, preferring to

remember when I met him in Anchorage last month for a beer, rather than the night we first met.

The agents leave, and Branson exhales heavily and curses. "Thanks for coming down."

"I didn't do much."

"Yeah, you did." He stands up. "Did I interrupt a date?" He glances at my clothes.

I shake my head and chuckle. "No, you didn't. I wanted to impress Sofie when I picked her up for dessert at your place."

"Oh, shit! I forgot."

"Don't worry about it. You have a lot on your plate right now." I pause and raise my eyebrows as we head out of the station. "So, what do you think of Adele?"

I receive a scowl in response to my question. "She's a fed."

I roll my eyes and drape an arm over his shoulders as we step outside. "She was checking you out."

"I don't need to know that." He shoves me away. "Give Sofie and Judean my apologies for tonight."

"I will, but they'll understand." I turn to Branson as I get in my truck. "Hey, I don't mind you calling me." I hold his gaze until he nods in acknowledgment. Then, I drive away, wondering why I always feel like I must remind him that I'm okay with being there for him.

Chapter Eighteen

Sofie

IT FEELS STRANGE TO BE WRAPPED IN A BLANKET WHILE sitting on Maddox's couch. The leather is soft and comfortable. It's too comfortable. My eyes are struggling to stay open. It isn't even ten o'clock. Time is deceiving here because there are only a few hours of darkness, and even then, it's not fully dark. I do like it here. It's peaceful. From the brief glimpse I've had, the town looks quaint. Can I imagine myself living here? Yes, I can. I think I could be happy in this small town with Maddox. He left me speechless when he asked me because I wasn't expecting it. But deep down, I knew the answer all along. My whole body comes alive when I think about Maddox. I've never felt this way about anyone before, and considering that I was engaged until recently, I'm not sure that I can trust my judgment. But oh, how I want to trust it! For once, I want to follow my fluttering heart instead of my head and take a chance on love with Maddox.

Love.

I'm not sure I'm ready for that yet. I've only known him for a very short time. I don't believe in love at first sight. Lust at first sight, however, is something I can get down with, because the second our eyes met, I felt a strong physical attraction.

Sighing into the sofa, I know I won't be getting naughty with the sexy man. Oh, I want to. Just not tonight since I'll be sleeping on his couch because he doesn't have a bed in the guest room. I'll have to resist the temptation and keep my thoughts in check.

"I've never had a woman wait for me before."

His voice startles me for a split second, and then I smile to myself. I rest my arms on the back of the sofa and look up at him coyly, feeling a rush of excitement. "I'm sure plenty of women have waited for you."

"You know what? You are absolutely right." He grins and moves from the doorway. "But only one, and that was my mom." His eyes soften as he moves closer and wraps me in a warm hug, joining me on the sofa.

I curl into his side. "Is everything okay?"

"It could be better." He sighs. "But I'm glad you're here with me. You gave me something to look forward to instead of my own company." He pauses. "Branson apologizes for canceling tonight."

I rest a hand on his chest and peer up into his eyes. "He has nothing to apologize for. He's the only sheriff around, right? That means he's always on the clock. Perhaps I could make lunch tomorrow and we could take it to him at the station."

"Speaking of which, your friend surprised me. I had no idea she wanted to stay here."

"Me neither. I think what Samantha said to her was the last straw. She wants and needs to be away from toxic people. Her father is friends with Samantha's dad, so it must be awkward for her. I'm glad she's going to stay. That means I'll have a female friend when I move here, too."

I'm sure he stopped breathing for a second. "What?" he asks, his voice thick and husky.

"We're not going to have hot and sweaty sex tonight, so don't get any ideas," I say with a smile. "But I said I want to move to Hawke's Ridge too. Maybe Judean and I can find a place to rent together."

"You can move in here with me."

"Maddox," I groan. "We don't even know each other."

"Of course we do." He pulls me onto his lap. I should have stayed still because wiggling on top of him means a hard, long, thick ridge is pressing between my legs. I gasp and push against his chest, but it's no use. "Stay still." He swallows hard. "I won't get us naked right now. I promise. Just don't wiggle that sexy butt in my lap, or I'm going to come in my pants like a horny kid."

I grin with a sparkle in my eye but settle down.

"I know the sound you make when you come. There's nothing more personal than that." He winks. "I know you were unhappy until you arrived in Alaska and met me. I know you like to read crime novels. You like some nonfiction as well. I also know you like your coffee black with no sugar. You wiggle your nose slightly when you're annoyed. I've noticed the way your eyes light up when you laugh, and how your mouth subtly curves when you smile." He softly brushes my hair away from my face and caresses my cheek. "I think I know quite a bit about you, Miss Ryan." He leans in and whispers, "I'm falling for you," and his lips gently brush along mine.

I close my eyes, overwhelmed with desire for this man. To my horror, a tear slips free, and I snap my eyes open. He reaches up and wipes it away with a soft smile on his face.

"You have opened my eyes to an exciting future. Your smile makes my knees weak. The way my body reacts when you touch me." I blush, but continue, "The way you are there for your brother when he needs you is admirable. The others, too. You have strong family values, and that means everything to me. I've never met anyone quite like you, and I'm selfish because I don't want to let you go."

"Well, babe, I don't plan on letting you go." He smirks. "I planned on following you to Frisco and bringing you back home to Hawke's Ridge." Clearing his throat, he adds, "Is that okay with you?"

"You don't need to follow me, although I wouldn't mind some help packing up and figuring out how to get everything here."

"Sure." His hands grip my hips. "Now, I think it's time for me to feel those lips on mine."

My heart catches in my throat as a wave of excitement and nerves washes over me. Scooting closer, I shudder at the feel of him hard and throbbing. His eyes flutter with lust as I lean in, closing the gap between us and finally pressing my lips against his. The kiss is slow and sweet. Languid. I reach up and caress his face, deepening the kiss as my tongue slips inside his mouth to dance with his. He moans softly, his hands moving to my waist and pulling me closer.

Hunger and desire race through me as I rub myself against his erection. His breathing quickens, and I feel his heart pounding against my chest.

The pulse between my legs quickens as I grind against him. His large hands on my hips help me move. "That's it," he coaxes. "Just like that." His hips rise and fall in time with mine. I feel every hard, throbbing inch of him against the lips of my pussy as he brings me closer to the edge.

"Oh," I moan.

"Come on me, Sofie. I want to watch you climax, knowing your wet pussy is desperate for my cock. I want to see you lose control and beg for it."

"Maddox," I moan, my head thrown back and my body

trembling with desire. His mouth latches onto my neck, and I come apart in his arms. My pussy pulses as I cry out his name. The pleasure is overwhelming, consuming me whole. I drop my head to his shoulder and enjoy his embrace while my heart slows. "I'll take care of you when I can move," I say. "You've given me two orgasms, and your balls must be blue."

He laughs deep and richly. "Babe, a sexy-as-fuck woman was rubbing my dick and making little whimpering sounds that had me coming in my pants."

My eyes widen. "You did?"

He smirks. "I need a shower."

I chew on my lip, debating how to answer the question he's silently asking. "Is there room for another?"

He winks and says, "I'll always make room for you."

Chapter Nineteen

Maddox

Sofie settles back into my arms and sighs into my chest. A gentle breeze ruffles our hair. I don't ever remember feeling so content. This morning, Sofie has my Harley between her legs as we stare at the valley below.

Last night, our slippery bodies teased each other, yet we didn't have sex. That doesn't mean we didn't get off. I smile to myself, remembering how it felt to have my hands all over a naked and very wet Sofie. My dick twitches behind my zipper, sending lust to my balls.

Bad idea.

I inhale deeply and brush my lips over the curve of her ear.

I know I've fallen hard for this woman. I never thought I'd see the day when I'd be obsessed with a woman. Last night, I respected her decision to wait a day before making love to her. Instead, I held her all night, happy that she was with me.

She turns her face into my neck, and I catch the sigh that passes her lips. "I don't know why I felt so obligated to wait a day," she admits. "I mean, a day is nothing. In my mind, I'd already broken up with Richard before he ever showed up in Alaska."

I press a kiss to the top of her head and say, "You're a good person, Sofie."

"I think I'm going to need you to pinch me every once in a while, because I still can't believe I'm moving to Alaska. To this wild and beautiful place."

I clear my throat.

Sofie chuckles. "You, Maddox Hawke, are the only reason I'm making this decision." She starts moving about. "Help me turn around."

Once she's settled, she runs her fingers through my short whiskers, smiling. "I've always loved Alaska from afar. It was never a place I considered living until I stepped off the plane. You had a lot to do with that need inside of me. You are the one who has given me the courage to take my life back. To make my own decisions instead of following someone else's plan for my life. I feel free when I'm with you." I chuckle. "I also feel a lot of things that will make me blush in public."

I laugh. "We're not in public."

"Maybe I'll tell you tonight when I have you naked and

under me," she teases. "I have a wicked tongue that I haven't put to use before."

I narrow my eyes, wondering if she means what I think she means. Oh, she does. The spark of excitement in her eyes tells me that we're on the same page. "How have you made it to twenty-six without giving head?"

"I haven't had that much sexual experience. My boyfriend before Richard would climax the second, I touched him. Richard said he doesn't like it." I shrug. "So, I get to practice my awesome sucking skills on you."

"Babe, if you don't stop talking about blowing me, I'm going to have jizz in my pants again."

"Don't you want to know how I know what to do?" Her eyes sparkle with mischief as I narrow mine.

"I'm afraid to ask."

Sofie places her hands on my thighs and moves them up to the bulge at my groin. I shudder when she drags the tip of a finger down my shaft. The tip of her pink tongue slips between her swollen lips. They're swollen because I can't stop kissing this beautiful woman.

A cheeky smirk appears on her face seconds before she unfastens my jeans. We both gasp when my erect penis jerks free of the denim. Arousal tingles up its length and pools on the head as Sofie watches, licking her lips.

"I feel like I'm going to jump out of my skin," I admit.

Sofie smiles, her eyes dark with desire. "Can I taste you?" she whispers, her voice full of hunger.

"Yes," I croak, barely recognizing my own voice.

Her small hand wraps around my large girth, and I shiver with anticipation. My balls tighten as she leans in closer. I watch her lip's part, ready to take me into her mouth. Her pink tongue comes out, and while holding my gaze, she swipes it over my slit, sending a shockwave of pleasure through me.

"Mmm, you taste really good." She whimpers. "I hope you're ready for this." Before I can reply, her mouth is on me. Not gentle. But rough and hungry. I surrender to the sensations, knowing I am at her complete mercy.

My legs quiver as Sofie takes me deep. Her nose tickles the hair around the base of my quivering cock. I slide my hands into her hair and gently guide her movements. The sight of her giving me head and the feel of her hot, wet mouth drives me crazy. It's a struggle to keep the bike steady because my legs quiver. I grip her hair as she starts bobbing up and down. Her hands come up and grab my hips, and I let out a deep moan of pleasure. "I'm close," I hiss, feeling the tension build inside me.

She only replies by sucking me hard and deep. Having her mouth on me feels amazing, and I don't want it to stop. I tighten my ass, trying to hold off my release for as long as possible. It doesn't work. Sofie moans, sending vibrations through my cock. "Fuck, Sofie! I can't hold off. I'm going to come."

I try to push her away, but she won't budge. Her mouth moves faster, determined to make me come, and I do. I explode into her mouth, grunting with pleasure as she sucks me dry. I groan deeply as I finish, my body tingling with pleasure.

Sofie gently pulls away and smiles up at me, knowing she made me lose my mind. "I guess I did that right, huh?"

I burst out laughing. "Babe, you did it so right that I'm struggling to keep the bike upright." My chest heaves as I pull her into my arms and hold her tightly. "As soon as we get back to my cabin, I'm going to show you just how much I appreciate your mouth." I smirk, and when she opens her mouth to speak, I don't give her a chance. I cover her mouth with a deep kiss that shows her how much I want her. She responds eagerly, melting into my embrace.

My heart sinks when I see Branson's truck parked outside my cabin. There goes my chance to spend the morning back in bed with the beautiful woman clinging tightly to me on my Harley.

He didn't want me at this morning's meeting with Gabe, which is why I took Sofie out on the bike. I pull onto my driveway and wait for Sofie to climb off before I do. I smile as I help her with the helmet fasteners, removing hers and then my own. I hang them on the handlebars and meet my brother's gaze.

"I always seem to be interrupting you." His eyes move to Sofie. "Sorry about that."

Sofie shakes her head. "You have nothing to apologize for. Can I make you a coffee? Have you eaten?"

"My brother has you right at home." He follows Sofie into the house while I bring up the rear.

"Maddox insisted that I get comfortable here and treat it like my home." She shrugs. "It feels odd, but I'm trying. Although, I will say, it's easier with you because you look like you need taking care of."

"I wouldn't go that far," I say, not liking where her thoughts are going.

Chuckling, she pours Branson a coffee and adds cream and two sugars. I raise an eyebrow, but she only smiles wider. "So, Branson, what can we do to help?"

"Fuck no!" I mutter. "I don't want you anywhere near the sheriff's station while that sick fucker is around."

Her eyes narrow. "I have a mind of my own, Maddox Jameson Hawke."

I wince, and so does my brother. "She's pulling out the full name." He snickers. "Best listen to her."

I run a hand through my hair. "Sofie, I'm not trying to be a jerk about this. I'm worried, okay? Any other time, if you want to hang out with one of my brothers, that's fine. But I just need to know you're safe."

Her face softens as she moves closer and wraps her arms around my waist. "I'll only go there if you're with me, okay?"

Still not liking that idea, I mumble, "Okay," and meet my brother's eyes. "What happened with Gabe?"

"That asshole is lying about something," Branson says

angrily. "He didn't give me a straight answer about what he was doing in Montana. I know him. He has a tell when he lies. I noticed it. I think Sheridan picked up on it, too."

"Why would he make shit up? He's not the one doing this."

"Wait?" Sofie straightens and faces Branson. "Gabe isn't involved in this. He was upset about it. He thought he should have done more to find her. Also, if he was doing this, wouldn't he make sure to have a perfect alibi?"

"He would." Branson frowns. "I want to know what he was actually doing there. When he was in Montana, he told us he was meeting friends in upstate New York."

"Fuck!" I curse.

"Oh," Sofie says quietly. "That's not good."

"No, it isn't," I agree. "This just got a lot more complicated."

Branson rubs his forehead. "I'd better get back to the office." He grins. "Judean is organizing the files and tidying up the office. Landon doesn't know what hit him."

"You need to utilize me and the others. Don't do anything alone, especially if we're after Bigfoot."

"Bigfoot?" Sofie asks, eyeing us both.

"A size fourteen boot print was found. It could be the killer or someone else." With a wince, Branson backs away. "I'll call when I need assistance."

We watch him leave and head inside the cabin. Sofia plops down on the arm of the sofa and removes her jacket and boots. "You know, there are eight of you plus your father.

Maybe Gabe just wanted some downtime where no one knew where he was." She shrugs. "I don't want to believe for a second that Gabe is the sick bastard killing women. I can't see him doing that. I mean, I have zero experience being around a killer, so maybe I'm wrong, but really? He has an amazing family, and Gabe is really nice."

"He's too gentle to hurt anyone," I add.

"People said that about Ted Bundy." Sofie slaps a hand over her mouth, and her eyes widen. "I'm so sorry. I don't know why that came out of my mouth."

I burst out laughing, although it isn't funny. "Babe, let's not talk about my brother or anything else." I move into her space and pull her into my arms.

Her legs wrap around my hips and her arms around my neck. "Are you going to do filthy things to me?"

Grinning, I walk us to my bedroom. "If you call eating your pussy filthy, then yes, I am." I toss her onto my bed. "Get naked."

I kick off my boots and socks and toss my T-shirt across the room. As I unbuckle my belt, I freeze when I watch Sofie wiggle out of her jeans and little lace panties. My mouth waters at the sight of her pussy, lightly covered with neatly trimmed hair. "Breathtaking," I mutter, my eyes roaming over her sexy legs, the curve of her hips, and her bared breasts.

Fuck me!

"Fucking gorgeous." I spread her legs and drop to my knees on the floor. Gripping her ankles, I pull her toward me.

I run my hands up along her thighs. She watches me with every touch. She shivers when I tweak her nipples.

"You forgot to remove something."

"If my dick touches you, I won't be able to control myself. I want you so fucking much," I admit. I spread her legs, tug some more, and put her gorgeous legs over my shoulders, her wide-open pussy in front of my face. "Babe, you're dripping."

I dip down, inhaling her scent, and moan as I use my tongue to slip between her swollen folds and take a taste. My heart pounds as Sofie lets out small whimpers of pleasure. Her hips rock and shove her pussy closer to my face. Not wanting to disappoint her, I grip her hips and kiss her pussy until she's squirming beneath me, her arousal flowing freely. She tastes like pure heaven. The moment I slip a finger inside her and suck her clit, she explodes, her whole-body quivering as she pulses on my finger.

One orgasm isn't enough for me, so I continue fingering and licking her. I know she's about to climax again when she grinds her pussy on my mouth, soaking my mouth and chin with her orgasm. I slip a hand down to my groin and release my aching cock. I stand up, kick my jeans away, and let my eyes rove over a sated Sofie. Her eyes travel over me, lingering on my cock. She licks her lips, meeting my gaze. "That looks painful."

I wrap a hand around my dick and do a shallow pump, feeling precum leaking out. "It's as hard as a rock and desperate to feel your tight, wet pussy milking it."

Opening herself to me, she holds out a hand. "Fuck me, Maddox."

"I'm clean. No sex for a long while." Sofie has been distracting me, so I can barely remember when I last had sex.

"I have the implant, so I can't get pregnant. I haven't had sex in forever."

Forever—she was engaged.

I put the thought out of my mind for now. With how hard my dick throbs, I take it in-hand and direct the tip inside Sofie, muttering under my breath. My eyes roll back in my head when Sofie's tight cunt sucks me inside her. I surround my woman, clamping a hand on her bottom and one on the back of her head. I seal our lips together as my body starts moving.

The kiss is deep and tender. I only break free for air. I smile down at her while thrusting into pure heaven. Shards of pleasure shoot back and forth along my spine as I ensure that my cockhead rubs against that sensitive spot inside her. Sofie moans each time I hit it.

My body feels alive, from the tips of my toes to the top of my head. Sofie reaches down and manages to grab my butt, digging her fingernails into my flesh. I tense and tighten my ass, making my dick turn to stone as I grind my pelvis against hers. Sofie stretches upward, giving me the chance to capture a breast in my mouth. I suckle and nibble on the hard, cherry-red nipple. But that's it. She's so tight in this position that I start coming without warning. Full-on orgasm. Sofie whimpers and shudders beneath me. Her body pulses around my dick, drawing out more semen as I experience a wave of pleasure that I don't want to end.

I rest my forehead against Sofie's and brush a sweet kiss over her lips. Then, panting hard, I grab her up in my arms, flip us over, and rest on my back so that I don't crush her. Lucky for me, my dick is still inside her, and the little pulses are making me hard again.

"That was out of this world. I thought the top of my head was going to blow off," she giggles. "You're not just hot, you're a sex god!"

"I can live with that," I reply with a smug grin. "Your pussy is made for me."

"And your dick belongs to me now."

I stare into her eyes, catching my breath at the emotion she's showing me. I never want this woman to leave.

We kiss until I'm hard as fuck. Sofie sits astride me and starts riding for all she's worth.

Chapter Twenty

Sofie

After spending the morning in bed with Maddox, my body feels energized. Just thinking about him without clothes makes me feel giddy and tingly. He's fit in all the right places, and he makes me happy just by being around him. I'm relaxed with him, and I never want this feeling to end.

I haven't ventured out to the main lodge yet, so I don't know what to expect. Richard will undoubtedly still be around because he expects everyone to say yes to him. I hadn't realized what a burden being engaged to him was until I'd given him his ring back. I feel so much lighter now, as though a mountain has been lifted from my shoulders. There is a twinge of guilt, though. I should never have let things get to this point. But I wouldn't have met Maddox if I'd gotten my act together sooner and ended things at home. I can't be sad about that.

Sighing, I finish wrapping the sandwiches to take to the sheriff's station. Considering there are two agents in town, I've made a good few. Branson looked tired last night, and I felt sorry for him because he has no one to take care of him. I figured I could do that until he has someone of his own.

I smile when I hear the door open and see Maddox stride inside. His eyes land on me, and then he's in my personal space with his hand on my face, leaning in for a kiss. It's sweet, tender, and slow, and it makes my heart ache with happiness. I lick my lips when he pulls away. "The sandwiches are ready."

"Hmm." He holds my gaze a moment longer. "We'll take the truck this time." He smirks.

My cheeks heat, and I try to duck my head, but Maddox won't let me. He catches my chin with a finger and brings my face upward to his. "Don't be embarrassed. We're together now. Nothing is embarrassing." He kisses my hot cheekbones and whispers, "I was thinking about what I can do to you later with my mouth, hands, and cock. Lots of filthy things come to mind."

I shudder and let out a small whimper. "You're naughty."

He laughs. "You called me a sex god earlier."

I roll my eyes. "I knew that would go to your head."

"I wonder which head you're referring to?" He raises his eyebrows, and I burst out laughing.

"I think we should head out for lunch before I drag you back to bed."

He laughs, hauls the box I've packed the lunch in, and settles it on his arm. Then he takes my hand. "Let's go."

"Okay. Did you speak to Gabe?"

"No, I can't find him, and he's not answering his phone."

I frown. "That's strange, isn't it?"

"As much as I hate to admit it, yes, it is. He usually has the phone glued to his hands, or at least within reach. Something doesn't add up, but I don't believe he has anything to do with the deaths," he says. He secures the box of food in his truck and lifts me into my seat. He places his hands on my knees. "He's my brother, Sofie. I know him. He didn't do this." With those final words, he gets into the truck and drives us into town.

"Fuck," he curses as we pull up to the sheriff's station. "I've got a bad feeling about this."

I follow his gaze and wonder what's going on. There are four men talking with a deputy. "Do you know them?"

"Deputy Landon. The other four were in the office the other day. Their sister saw someone behind where they're staying. That's how we found Andrea."

I follow him out of the truck, but I stay back when he approaches the men. Their discussion seems angry.

"You need to find her!" A large man snaps the second he notices Maddox.

"I just arrived, so start from the beginning," Maddox says.

Another man steps in. "My sister has disappeared. Her phone is in her room. She never goes anywhere without her phone. Not even to the bathroom. Her suitcase has been knocked over, and her clothes are scattered across the floor. She's OCD about being tidy. She can't have anything lying around. She saw the creep behind the B&B, and now something has happened to her."

"You have to find her," another man begs.

Maddox rubs his chest and looks my way. "Can you go tell Branson what's going on?"

I nod and quickly head inside the station. Judean stands behind the reception desk amidst files. Her face lights up when she spots me. "We'll catch up soon, but I need to talk to Branson right now. Where is he?"

"In his office."

I stare, not having a clue where that is.

"Back there. You can't miss it. The feds are with him."

"I think they're needed, too." I rush past a frowning Judean and follow the soft sound of voices. I knock, then enter and find Branson behind his desk with a deep frown on his face. "Maddox and Landon are outside. The girl who reported the man behind the B&B has disappeared."

His eyes widen as he jumps to his feet. He grabs his hat. "Sofie, stay with Judean."

I nod.

Branson and the two agents head outside.

"A girl's gone missing," I tell Judean, explaining what's

going on. I slouch on the counter between us. "Great first day, huh?"

"I'm used to emergencies and officers running out of the building. I suspect it's unusual here, though."

"How's it going otherwise? Are you organizing the station?"

She smiles, her eyes dancing. "I am. Whoever had this job before me wasn't very organized." She moves closer and whispers, "I already love this job. Branson will be a great boss. Landon is lazy. I discovered that within thirty minutes of being here. But I really like it here, Sofie. The town. The brothers. Some of the townspeople have even come by to welcome me. I met Angie and Bud. They invited me to their bar for a drink on the house." She smirks. "Angie told me the single guys hang out there, too."

"Hmph," I mutter. "What about Colton?"

"What about him?" Judean doesn't meet my gaze.

"Seriously, *Juju*," I grin. "That man has the hots for you."

Her eyes narrow at the nickname. "He wants anyone with a pussy."

A loud throat clears behind us. Judean snaps her gaze over my shoulder, and I slowly turn, knowing Branson is the one who overheard her.

"We brought sandwiches," I say, redirecting his gaze. "Lots of them. Maddox called in an order for a couple of flasks of coffee from Patricia's."

"Nice change of subject," he comments.

I roll my eyes. "She," I say, pointing over my shoulder, "was referring to your youngest sibling."

"Thank God for that." He turns his gaze to Judean. "I'm heading out with Landon, and the feds. You can reach us on the radio or cell."

"Okay, boss," Judean says.

"Will you be okay here alone?" Branson pauses.

"I'll be here, so she won't be alone." I shrug. "I'm not doing anything Samantha planned, so I can stay and help Judean get organized."

"Okay." He backs out of the office, and I turn to face Judean. "I bet he tells Colton what you said."

She scoffs. "No way. Branson doesn't gossip like his brothers do."

"I wouldn't be so sure about that."

"Why is this filed under 'M'?" I ask, not understanding the previous filing system at all.

Judean lifts her head from the file she's reading. "What name is on it?"

"Joshua Pearler."

"Huh. Well, your guess is as good as mine."

Our eyes move to the door as Landon steps inside. I turn to him and ask, "Do you know why this is filed under M?" I hold it out to him, and he takes it from my hand.

He scans the cover quickly before replying, "He killed his wife, Melanie."

My eyes flicker to Judean, who shrugs and quickly buries her face in the file she's engrossed in.

"Oh, well, that makes sense."

He looks at me as though he can't decide if I'm serious or being sarcastic. I hold his gaze, trying to keep my expression neutral. Huffing out a breath, he moves toward the back of the station.

"Does that make sense to you?" I ask Judean.

"Well, if I'm the one filing and retrieving, then perhaps. Pearler isn't the only file out of place. It's such a mess. How anyone is expected to find anything in these cabinets is a mystery." Judean plops down beside me and sighs in frustration. "I just started this job, and I like it. Once everything has been filed correctly, it won't be so difficult."

"From your mouth to God's ears," I mutter.

Judean snickers. "If only." Her stomach growls at that moment.

"Oh! I forgot. Lunch is in the truck. Let me go get it." I hand Judean the file and head outside.

Maddox stands beside his brother, who is writing in a notepad. He sees me and breaks away from the group. He leans in close and says, "This isn't good, Sofie." I search his eyes and see only worry. I step into his space and wrap my arms around him. He buries his face in my shoulder, seeking comfort.

Brushing a kiss across my lips, he puts his arm around my

shoulders and leads me to his truck. "I'm going with Branson to organize a search for Olly Denver. I'll leave the keys to my truck with you. When you're done with Judean, drive her back to the lodge, okay? I'd rather you not be on foot."

"You're really worried."

"This guy is escalating." He holds my face in his hands and gently rests his forehead against mine. "I need you and Judean to be safe."

"Okay. Please don't worry about me. Take care of yourself." I kiss him and say, "I need to get the sandwiches out of the truck."

"I forgot about those." He gets them himself, and I follow him back into the office. "I'm going to take two for me and Branson." He kisses me again, puts the keys to his truck in my hand, and leaves.

"They're going to search for Olivia Denver. I really hope they find her unharmed."

"This is awful. That poor girl. Do you think we should join the search?"

"Yes, if they ask for volunteers. For now, though, Maddox wants us to finish up here and head back to the lodge. He's worried about our safety."

"That's why I'm here," Colton says to our surprise, stepping into view.

"Where did you come from?" I ask, drawing his gaze from Judean.

"I'm parked around back. I came in that way."

"Why are you here?" Judean asks, her hands on her hips.

"Babe, you and Sofie are alone here. There's a killer on the loose. I'm sticking to you like glue until he's caught." Colton leans against the wall, crosses his arms over his chest, and rests a booted foot against it. If I weren't with Maddox, I'd be drooling.

Judean tries to appear indifferent, but I notice her sidelong glances at Colton. I'm sure he does too, judging by the spark of desire in his eyes when he looks at her.

Judean's stomach grumbles again, this time loudly enough for Colton to hear. He straightens against the wall. Before he can open his mouth, I blurt out, "Sandwiches!" Reaching inside the box, I pull out three wrapped sandwiches and hand them out. "Colton, come and sit with us. Oh! Where did Landon go?"

"He's hiding in the back," Colton hisses, shaking his head in disgust. "Landon, lunch is here," Colton shouts.

His footsteps announce his arrival, and Colton nods toward the box of food. I add, "There's a sandwich in there for you. Nothing fancy, just chicken and mayonnaise."

"Thank you."

The door bursts open. "Landon." Branson narrows his eyes at his deputy. "I sent you the address. Head out now." He pauses when he spots Colton but does an about-face. Landon shoves his hat onto his head, sighs loudly, and takes the sandwiches with him as he follows Branson outside.

I turn to Colton. "Why is he a deputy when it's obvious he doesn't want to do anything?"

"Branson inherited him from his predecessor." Colton

shrugs. "He needs to send the guy to a refresher course in Anchorage." Pause. "Either that or a kick up the ass."

I ignore the latter. "Surely, he can't have forgotten his training. He doesn't look like he's worn the uniform for that long."

"He's close to thirty, I think. He's been a deputy since he turned nineteen, from what I heard." He takes a huge bite of the sandwich and starts to chew. "I'm not sure why he's so lazy." Colton continues to eat while deep in thought.

Judean smirks at me and asks, "So, you've moved in with Maddox, huh?"

"As you know, Richard showed up last night. He insisted on staying in my room. There was no way I was going to stay there. Maddox insisted." I offer her a small smile as I feel my cheeks start to heat up. "He's a good man."

"I agree." Judean says. "There aren't many places to rent here."

Colton goes still, which draws our gaze. Judean asks, "What's wrong?"

"Are you staying in Hawke's Ridge?"

Judean grins. "We are!"

"Don't worry about finding a place. Maddox said you can move into his guest room," I add.

"Uh, no way! You can move in with me."

Judean and I both give Colton our full attention, and, for once, I notice him squirm in his seat. "You're a horn-dog, and you expect me to move in with you?" Judean asks.

"You are not moving in with Maddox."

"Sofie," she says, pointing my way, "is Maddox's girl. I'll be in the guest room." She asks me, "Are you sure he won't mind?"

"He offered." I smile.

"Not happening," Colton states, then smiling. "You can move in with my dad!" he says, snapping his fingers. "Ugh! Moms supposed to be coming here." He winces. "I'm not sure that's a good idea."

"Look, I can stay with Sofie and Maddox until I find a place," Judean says.

"Babe, if you think I'm going to let you sleep with my brother, then you don't know me very well."

Sensing an argument about to start, I jump into the fray. "You," I say, pointing to Colton, "need to listen. She will be sleeping alone. I'll be sleeping with your brother. Now, stop acting like a Neanderthal and help us finish this filing so we can be done with it. I hate filing."

He grumbles some more, then mutters, "I don't have the hots for *anyone* with a pussy."

I burst out laughing, and Judean turns bright red. I snicker and avoid her gaze.

Chapter Twenty-One

Maddox

AGENTS ADELE AND KALLUK WORK WELL TOGETHER. THEY are efficient and work at a fast pace. All this sucks. Branson seems to have slipped back into his old detective ways. It's something he hasn't had to do since he moved here. I'm relieved he's found his way back, but I'm not too happy about the reason why.

I rub a hand across my face, thinking about my brother, Gabe. He's been quiet, and no one has seen him since Branson and the feds interviewed him this morning. I know it worries Branson. Still, Gabe isn't responsible for what's going on. When he tells the truth about his whereabouts, that will be clear. Until then, the feds have doubts about him. I don't blame them.

He's acting like an asshole, and I'm angry with him for being evasive. The feds could be looking elsewhere, but Gabe is on their minds as they wonder why he's lying.

Frustration eats away at me as I pace behind my brother's truck. Landon sits in his patrol car while Branson and the agents talk amongst themselves.

Hunter strides toward me in his deputy uniform. "Dad told Mom," he says. "Now she's worried and crying."

"Mom didn't need to know anything yet," I grumble.

Hunter puffs out a loud breath and curses. "He did it to get Mom here. You know that, right? It worked, too. She's booked a flight." Pause. "Although, from what I gathered, she'd already booked the flight after a conversation about you and your trouble with women. So, I guess we can't really blame Dad."

"I don't have trouble with women. I was just looking for advice on how to get one woman. She's mine now," I add with a smile, tilting my lips. "I miss Mom." I sigh and look out over the forest. "But this is not the time to visit."

"I doubt Dad will let her leave the cabin, so she'll be safe enough."

I wince at his words, and Hunter catches me, smirking. "They'll only be doing what you and Sofie are."

"Don't be such an asshole," I say, shaking my head to get rid of the thought.

"Should we join them?" He nods toward the group.

"I was waiting for you."

He snickers. "Pussy!"

I give him the finger as we turn and head toward the group. When we get close, the first thing out of Branson's mouth is, "Where's Landon?"

"In his car," Hunter answers.

Branson glances over our shoulders. "He's on his way." Sigh. "Landon!" he roars. "I want you to search the west side with Hunter." He turns to me and says, "You'll double up with Kalluk and take the east side. Sheridan and I will head north. Olivia's father, Daniel, and her brothers, Scott, Jason, and Lyle are searching too. I've loaned each of them a fluorescent vest. Stay in touch by radio."

I nod, relieved that I don't get paired with Landon. However, Hunter hasn't unclenched his jaw since Branson laid out the assignments. We each take a radio and check in.

"Her name is Olly, short for Olivia," Branson adds. "We're not doing this quietly, so call out. Make as much noise as you can. The rangers are keeping everyone away today. That doesn't mean a hunter or two hasn't bypassed them. So be vigilant."

I grab a fluorescent vest and clip the radio to it.

Branson grabs my arm. "Are you armed?"

"Yes."

"Good." He shuts his vehicle up tight and, after saying something to Sheridan they head out.

I glance at Kalluk and see that the agent is ready to go. "I know the area."

He nods. "Let's go."

Hunter waves Landon in front of him, and the officer reluctantly heads out. My brother glances at me over his shoulder. I wave, knowing it will annoy him. "Is there a story behind the deputy?"

"Honestly, I'm not sure what's going on with him. The sheriff has tried to find out, but Landon remains the same."

"He needs a deputy who can back him up, but I don't see Landon reacting that quickly."

"No," I sigh. "It's a worry."

Ten minutes later, we're crunching through layers of twigs and leaves, and sweat trails down my back. The weather is hot and muggy, with hardly any breeze. Every so often, we stop and shout for Olly. Then, we listen closely for a response. Nothing. I have a sick feeling in my stomach that the killer has her. Maybe he thinks she saw more than she did. I hope my gut is wrong.

Suddenly, a flock of birds take to the sky. "There's something up ahead. Man, or animal. I have no idea."

He nods, accepting my word. "Hunters?"

"Could be. It could be one of us as well. Or something more deadly." I wince as the words leave my mouth. "Let's keep going but be more aware."

We move deeper into the forest where areas of shade and sunlight become scarce. The smell of pine and foliage is familiar. Piercing thorns dig into my skin as I push through the dense underbrush, which tangles and grabs at me. My heart races with fear of what we might find if we locate Olly. I try to push thoughts of danger out of my mind and focus on the task at hand. It's easier knowing that Sofie is safe with Judean and Colton. I wince, knowing Judean might not be impressed by my texting an SOS to my brother.

The sound of Kalluk's heavy breathing has me looking over at the man. "It's been a long time since I've trekked through a forest," he says after a moment.

Keeping my eyes on our surroundings, I ask, "How long have you and Sheridan worked together?"

"Two years." He huffs out a laugh. "She finished her probation and was assigned to me when the cross-state murders hit the bureau." He chuckles. "When she gets stuck into something, she won't let it go until it's finished to her satisfaction. I'm glad she has my back. I don't think I've ever trusted anyone as much as I trust her." He smiles wryly. "She reminds me of my sister, Jonny's mom. A firecracker."

I smirk. "Should I be worried about my brother?"

The agent has a twinkle in his eye. "There are going to be a lot of fireworks there."

"That's my take. Ready to go on?"

He nods.

"Ahead, the trail passes between sheer rock faces. It's narrow, but only around ten feet long."

Kalluk pats me on the back. "I got it."

The agent keeps up and appears less winded after resting for a few minutes. The overgrown section comes into view and the trail seems to disappear, but it doesn't. I found that out on my first hike in this area. My clothes are sticky with sweat as I lead Kalluk through the dense foliage and out into the open space between the two rock faces.

"I see what you mean about it being narrow," Kalluk comments.

"We should call in our location because we might lose all signal for an hour or so on the other side."

"I'll do it."

After taking a drink of water, I wait until Kalluk has finished talking on the radio before heading along the narrow path. I hear noise and glance up just in time to see rocks start to tumble down the rock face. "Move!" I shout, dashing through the passage. "Fuck!" The exit is blocked by a huge boulder. "We need to go back."

I quickly remove my backpack and hold it above my head as my eyes trail upwards. Kalluk does the same, turns around, and heads back the way we came. More stones tumble down and hit hard. "Stay close to the wall!" I yell over the noise, trying to shield myself from the falling rocks.

We break free of the passageway, and I quickly grab Kalluk by the arm and drag him away. Seconds later, with a loud roar, another large boulder falls from the sky and lands where Kalluk had been standing. Dust and debris fill the air as we catch our breath, grateful to have narrowly escaped a potentially deadly situation. The sound of falling rocks slowly fades.

I yank my radio free of the vest and manage to reach

Branson. After I explain the situation, he and Sheridan head our way. "We need to get up top," I tell Kalluk. "That wasn't an accident."

"No shit!"

I huff out a laugh. "Ready?"

Chapter Twenty-Two

Sofie

I SNAP A BREADSTICK IN HALF AND POINT ONE END TOWARD Colton, who is behind the reception desk now that we are back at the lodge. "You know, he's a really attractive man. I've always been a sucker for a guy in black pants and a white button-down."

"Will you stop pointing out his hotness? I want to know his weakness," Judean says, munching on her own breadstick.

"We both know his weakness is you," I point out, but she avoids my gaze. I snort in amusement. "I think he's cute."

"You think all the Hawke men are cute!"

"That is true." I smirk. "Maddox is the hottest by far."

She snorts. "Well, I'm staying away from Hawke men." She eyes Colton. "Especially the one sleeping his way through the town and lodge."

I frown. "I don't think that's as accurate as you've been led to believe."

"I know you like him, and you think it's hot to have him chase me, but he's too hot and delicious to really want me."

Our meals are placed in front of us, breaking into the conversation. I want to argue with her about her opinion of herself. It makes me sad that she doesn't see herself the way others do. I'm not going to point that out to her right now, but I need to help her become more positive about the way she looks. She's so cute with her Marilyn Monroe curves and boobs.

"I know you're upset over there, but I'm okay, Sofie." She pops a fry into her mouth. "I'm not the little kid who got called out for being fat in school. I know kids can be hateful. So can some adults." She glances over my shoulder, so I follow her gaze and my heart sinks. She mutters under her breath, "Speaking of the devil," and puts on a fake smile.

I take a hefty bite of my burger as they approach. Richard winces, and Samantha gives me a repulsive look. I nearly choke when Judean takes a huge bite of her burger and starts chewing with her cheeks bulging.

I close my eyes and force calm while I manage to swallow my food. I open my eyes again and drink water to wash the food down. I smile. "Are you having a good time, Richard?"

The brother and sister narrow their eyes. Samantha hisses,

"How do you expect my brother to have a good time when you won't talk to him?" Huffing out a loud breath, she adds, "Where did you sleep last night? I know it wasn't with Judean."

"How do you know she didn't sleep in my room?" Judean asks suspiciously. "You wouldn't be spying on me now, would you?"

"Don't be ridiculous." Samantha drops her eyes to the food, then to Judean. "You're never going to lose all that weight if you keep eating junk food."

Even Richard grows tense and frowns at his sister, but I can't contain my anger. I jump to my feet just as Colton slides into the chair next to Judean. He winks at her, saying, "Babe, you need plenty of substance for later, so eat up." He puts his arm around her shoulders and faces Samantha. "You could use a little more meat on your boobs. Guys like a woman to have dips and curves, something to hold on to while we fuck!"

My mouth drops open. I try to swallow my laughter. I really do. Yet I end up making such a gurgling noise that all eyes turn my way. I meet Judean's gaze and notice that she's bright red with either embarrassment or about to burst into tears.

Hell!

I jump to my feet. "Juju, let's head out." I shoot Colton a pointed glare and quickly glance at Judean. Thank God he gets my message and quickly stands, pulling Judean with him.

"Don't leave yet. Just one minute." He whispers something into Judean's ear, then dashes toward the kitchen. She shrugs.

"He's rude!" Richard says. "We need to make a formal complaint."

"Bullshit!" I hiss, surprising them. "Samantha has been rude to Judean since we arrived. It's been going on for a long time. So do not take the high road with me, Richard."

Colton returns and offers us both boxes for our food. I scoop mine up, happy that my food won't go to waste. Not only that, but I'm also hungry after working at the sheriff's station all afternoon. At least it kept my mind off Maddox for a few hours.

Once we have our food boxed up, I grab my jacket and start to move away from the table and the uninvited guests. However, Richard grabs my arm. "Sofie, can we please talk?"

Guilt seeps into my skin, and I find myself agreeing, "Tomorrow morning."

He opens his mouth to object—at least, I think that's what he was going to do—but then he nods.

"I can meet you in the breakfast room at nine, if that suits."

"I'll be there." Richard gives me a forlorn glance, and I swallow hard, hating myself for putting that look on his face. He is a good man, and I realize that I've treated him badly. He doesn't deserve that.

Judean takes my arm and leads me out of the restaurant. "I'm a horrible person," I mumble to her. "I treated Richard badly. The way I ended things."

"Before we arrived in Alaska, would you have broken up with him?"

"Yes." I sigh, not needing to think about it. "But for this trip being dropped in my lap, I would have admitted to Richard that I couldn't marry him. I don't love him, Judean."

"Then you have no reason to feel guilty." Judean directs me outside into the garden before stopping suddenly. "I forgot that you lost your room."

I smile and say, "I have a better one now."

"I bet you do." She snorts. "Also, if you call me Juju again, we can't be friends."

I snicker as I loop my arm through hers. "Let's go sit on the back deck and finish our food."

"You know, I really do like it here. The clean, breathable air. It's a nice change from city smog." Judean sighs. "No horns blaring, no traffic jams. Just peace and quiet."

As we come out through the kissing trees, it feels like we're in a whole other world compared to the lodge.

"Put me down, you big oaf!"

We stop and watch Bryant settle a woman over his shoulder. A large hand lands on her bottom. The woman squeals, and Bryant laughs and gives her a playful squeeze. That's when he notices Judean and me standing there, watching.

"My wife is home to stay!"

"Ah," I comment. "Carry on, then!"

"Tell our boys not to disturb us for a week."

"Oh, you, you—"

We miss what else she was about to say as they disappear inside his cabin.

I burst out laughing.

"The Hawke men are hot!" Judean mutters.

"You have a sexy Hawke man after you." I raise an eyebrow, but she ignores me. "Seriously, Judean, what's wrong with Colton? The man has a crush on you."

"He's horny as hell," Judean finishes with a smirk. "He isn't picky," she adds. "He'd probably sleep with a tree if it had a hole in it."

I frown, not liking where this conversation is going. "Judean, he practically drools every time he sees you. I think he really has a thing for you." I pause and take her hand. "Don't assume he only wants you for one thing." I pat her hand. "Why don't you ask him out to dinner?" I shrug and lead us up to Maddox's cabin. "Point out that it's only dinner and see what he says. I bet he'll agree within seconds."

"Hmph, maybe." Judean inches forward, then heads out onto the back deck.

Standing on the balcony, I enjoy the sound of chirping birds and rustling leaves, which is truly therapeutic. Gazing down toward the ravine hundreds of feet below, I smile to myself. The thought of living here fills me with happiness. I really hope Judean calms down and realizes how much Colton likes her. I don't think he's only after sex. Not the way he looks at her.

A slamming door from the front of the cabin makes me jump. Within a heartbeat, Gabe appears in the doorway, surprised to see us. He winces. "I was looking for Maddox."

The man looks a little worse for wear, so I move over and

grab his arm. "Come sit down, Gabe. Are you hungry?" I give him no choice but to join us.

"I'm fine." He drags a hand down his face. "I've messed up, Sofie." He glances toward Judean, then focuses on me.

"Bathroom?" my friend says.

I smile and give her brief directions before looking at Gabe. "How?"

He huffs out a breath. "I didn't tell the feds what I was really doing in Montana. It was obvious to anyone that I was lying."

"I don't understand." I sit forward. "Why would you need to lie?" The man before me is clearly not the killer, but there is obviously something else going on with him. "Gabe, let me help you. Let Maddox help you." I grip his hand. "You came here to talk to him, right? Talk to me. I don't believe for one minute that you had anything to do with Andrea's death." The silence stretches until I ask, "Why were you in Montana?"

"I visited someone in prison." His eyes hold mine as he waits for my reaction, but I don't give him one. "He's a killer." He sits forward and drops his head into his hands, looking defeated.

I move closer and tentatively place an arm around his shoulders to offer my support. "No matter why you were visiting him, I don't believe you're a killer. I know your brothers haven't wavered in their support of you, which is good enough for me. Now, get it all out, and we'll decide what to do."

He lifts his head, and I see that his eyes are rimmed red. My heart goes out to him. Slowly pulling himself together, he says in a slow, subdued voice, "He would drain his victims—all women—of enough blood to create a gruesome crime scene but not enough to kill them. Then, he would put them in a chest freezer and leave them to suffer until they died." He swallows hard. "That's what I think the killer is doing here. But, as God is my witness, I am not the one doing this. I haven't killed anyone. I swear it." He pauses. "But you see how it would look if I admitted to the feds what I was really doing in Montana?"

I frown. "Was the man a friend?"

His eyes widen, and he sits back in the chair, breaking our eye contact. "God, no!" He shakes his head. "I wrote a book about a serial killer in Texas when I was twenty. It was a best-seller at the time. A publisher approached me about writing one about Alex Piedmont. I turned him down initially. I didn't want all the publicity that comes with writing such a book. Ultimately, I decided to reach out to the killer and see where it led. I hadn't told anyone.

This sounds bad for Gabe, but I'm sure there must be a way to prove that he was elsewhere when the girls in Montana went missing. "You need to talk to Branson. He's your brother, as well as the sheriff. He'll have ways of tracking down information. What if you were checked in at the prison when one of the girls went missing? Let him help you. You could also get a lawyer to be with you when you tell the feds why you were there and why you initially lied."

Gabe nodded, a glimmer of hope appearing on his face at the suggestion. "Branson might be able to pull up the records from the visits to the prison," he says, wincing. "It could also backfire."

"You won't know until you try. But Gabe, you need to be honest with them because they will find out, and then it will look worse for you."

"I think I'm fucked either way."

Chapter Twenty-Three

Maddox

DRIPPING WITH SWEAT, I REMOVE THE BANDANA FROM around my head and wipe my face and neck as best I can. I wish I could take a shower right now. Even a heavy downpour would be welcome. I take a step back while Branson and the Feds discuss things. Kalluk and I didn't see or hear anyone. It was difficult to hear anything, though, with the roar of the avalanche of rock tumbling down on us. If someone was up here, they did a good job of hiding their presence.

The conversation ends just as the radio crackles to life. "Sheriff," Hunter says. "We've found a body." Pause. "Come to our location. Call in Janice and the team. Over."

"Fuck," Branson curses before replying, "Copy that. Over."

"I want you and Kalluk to head back to the truck." He turns to the agent and asks, "Can you make the call to Janice and get her moving?"

"Will do." Kalluk dabs at a deep gash on his hand before fastening a bandage around it.

"You both need to get those cuts taken care of, especially you." Branson nods at Kalluk, then at me and adds, "You look rough. Drop Kalluk off at the medical center, then go home and see your girlfriend. We're going to be overflowing with people soon. We've got it. Thanks, bro."

Relieved that he's dismissing me, I nod, yet I hesitate to leave him. "What about Olly's family?"

He sighs. "Unfortunately, they will have heard the radio."

I wince, feeling incredibly sorry for the family. I rub my forehead and hold my brother's gaze. "Call if you need me."

Branson gives me a tired nod.

Sheridan hands me more gauze and a bandage, and I wrap Kalluk's hand as well as I can. "That should hold."

"The rockslide was man's fault," he says. "What I don't understand is what the bastard gained from that. Nothing, as far as I can see. Not when he left Olly elsewhere for us to find."

"Unless we were getting close to where he was keeping the women."

Upon hearing this, Kalluk stares in my direction, and I get an uneasy feeling. The man smiles. "Branson said there's another way around the path we took. It's worth a look while we're here." He heads off in the direction that Branson and Sheridan went, but then he stops and looks embarrassed. "After you."

I snort. "We need to get to the trucks. You make the call to Janice, and I'll drive you to the hospital."

Cursing, Kalluk trudges behind me.

"I TAKE IT YOU'RE NOT GOING BACK TO THE B&B?" I ASK Kalluk. He just had eight stitches and was told to clean up before applying the thick dressing to his hand.

He winces. "I'd rather be on scene with Sheridan, but I know your brother has her back." He follows me out of the emergency room. "I'll drive the SUV up the mountain once I've cleaned up."

"I'm desperate for a shower. I stink."

Kalluk huffs out a laugh. "Then I'm in good company."

We stay silent until I drive past the sheriff's station, where my eyes linger.

"Has your woman finished up?" Kalluk asks.

"She has." I glance at Kalluk, then return my gaze to the road. "Sofie. It's her friend Judean who works there." I chuckle. "Today was her first day."

"The sheriff mentioned."

I pull up beside the feds' ride and wait for him to exit, but he sits, contemplating. "Talk to your brother." His eyes meet mine. "He lied to us. It doesn't look good for him." He climbs out and heads inside.

Gabriel is a jerk for lying to the feds. If he was going to do that, he could have at least prepared a convincing lie.

On the drive back to the lodge, my heart lightens at the thought of seeing Sofie. But at that thought, a wave of sadness washes over me, knowing Olivia Denver is dead. The poor girl. She had her whole life ahead of her. Like Andrea and the others.

Tired and smelling of sweat, I wince as I exit my truck. I glance at my cabin, and there she is: Sofie is standing on the small front porch, watching me with a sense of relief. I walk closer and hold up my hand to keep her away. "I stink."

She smirks and rolls her eyes. "You're not getting in the shower until you kiss me hello."

My face splits into a smile as I approach her and kiss her on the cheek. "Seeing you here does something to me. Waiting for me."

"I love being here," she whispers, going up on her tip toes and pressing her lips to mine. "Get in the shower. You have two minutes to soak before I join you."

I quickly remove my hiking boots and leave them upside down on the boot rack beside the front door. I then stride into the cabin. She follows behind me, and I hear the locks on the front door click into place. No interruptions.

In the bathroom, I toss my clothes into the hamper. I'm standing in the shower when the water starts to flow. I take a deep breath as the water meets my heated, sweaty body. It soon works wonders as I load a washcloth with shower gel and quickly get clean. Now I smell of roses, which is ten times better.

Out of the corner of my eye, I see Sofie join me. Her naked body brushes against my back, sending shivers down my spine. "Let me," she whispers as she grabs the bottle of shower gel. She brings her soapy hands to my chest and rubs the suds into my skin. My nipples harden as she plays with them before her sexy fingers wander much lower and wrap around my cock.

"Fuck, Sofie," I hiss, shivering at her slow stroke.

Her lips brush the top of my spine before her tongue comes out and traces a path down my back. "I love your ass."

I smirk, but it turns into a grunt when she lightly bites my buttocks, making my dick hard as a rock. "Oh," she mutters as she falls to her knees. I reach back, grasp a fistful of her hair, and tilt her head back. I turn to face her, almost coming when she squeezes my dick tightly.

"Open for me," I instruct. She licks her lips and obediently opens her mouth. I slide my cock in, feeling her throat clench around me as she takes me deeper. My legs quiver as she sucks me off with such intensity. Her hands latch onto the backs of my thighs, sliding upward to land on my buttocks. She digs her fingers into my flesh and moans in pleasure, sending shivers straight to my balls. I feel myself losing control with each passing second.

Her mouth moves to the tip, where she swirls her tongue around the engorged head. "I need you inside me."

I pull her up and kiss her deeply. My hands roam over her body, feeling every curve and dip, and my desire for her grows stronger. "I can't wait any longer." My cock pushes for entrance, and then it's surrounded by pulsating, wet heat. I lock my knees to keep them from buckling. Our lips crash together in a desperate, fiery kiss.

"Fuck me, Maddox. Hard and fast." I thrust into her, releasing all my pent-up desire and need. Her moans fill the room, driving me to move faster and deeper. The sound of our bodies colliding echoes in the air. "Oh!" Sofie lets out a keening wail as her orgasm pulsates through her, bringing my own climax to the surface. Thick streams of semen shoot out of my dick with each burst of pleasure, Sofie's vagina milks me for all it's worth. I feel the warmth of her skin against mine. Our breathing is ragged as we come down from an amazing high.

My hands are on Sofie's naked ass, and I don't want to let her go. My cock feels right at home nestled inside pure heaven. I drop a kiss onto her shoulder and nuzzle her neck, dipping down to suck one of her breasts into my mouth. She shudders in reaction, arching into my touch. Her fingers slide through my hair as she holds me close. "If you keep doing that, I'm going to need you to make me come again."

I let her breast pop out of my mouth and grin mischievously. "Challenge accepted."

Chapter Twenty-Four

Sofie

Feeling delightfully sated, I stretch my arms above my head and let out a small moan. Then, I settle back into the soft pillows on the bed. I gaze at Maddox's bare back, then his sculpted buttocks, and finally his strong legs. He's very nicely proportioned. I find I can't look away from the man. I'm also waiting for a full frontal.

My brows furrow when I notice his shoulders slump and he rubs his neck. Whatever he's being told is clearly not good news. Sliding out of my comfortable position, I grab one of his shirts from the open closet and slip it on. On my way past,

I grab a pair of his sweatpants, and then I pad softly over to him. He meets my gaze and holds out an arm to me. I go straight into his embrace, holding him close while he finishes talking with his brother.

He gives me a comforting squeeze before letting me go and taking the sweats, which he quickly puts on. "Thanks."

"What happened?"

"I assumed the body that Hunter found was Olivia." He sigh and runs a hand through his hair. "Turns out it wasn't her. She's still missing. They have no idea who the woman is who is currently on her way to the medical examiner's office."

"This is really bad," I say.

Maddox kisses me, takes my hand, and leads me into the kitchen. I jump onto a stool at the counter and smile as he pulls things out of the refrigerator. "Branson has Colton, Spencer, and Hunter helping with the search. He wants us— me, Ryland, and Garrett—to keep an eye on the lodge." He rests his hands on the countertop. "That means I want you to sleep in the lodge tonight. Share Judean's room, and keep it locked. You're not going anywhere alone."

I nod slowly, chills running through me at the seriousness of the situation. "I promise we'll stay together. I don't want you to worry about me."

I see in his eyes that he's still going to worry either way. I'll worry about him as well. "Oh, do you know your mom's here?"

He quickly blinks. "What?"

"Sorry for the sudden change of topic. I saw your dad carry her into his cabin earlier. He said not to disturb them for a week."

Maddox shudders. "That's good."

I snort. "You're full of shit! I can see how much the thought of your parents having sex bothers you. They have years to make up for."

"You need to stop!"

I tease, snickering, "I need something in my mouth to keep me quiet."

His eyes darken, and I raise my eyebrows. "I was thinking of an apple. I wonder where your mind went?"

"You know exactly where my mind was." He moves around the counter, cups the back of my head, and holds me while devouring my mouth. My body comes alive, relishing the dizzying heat of his mouth on mine, but then it's gone again.

"Hold that thought." He starts chopping vegetables and motions for me to sit and watch. "The staff will make sure the guests know there's a threat about town. I hope it doesn't reach here, but who knows? As far as I know, this asshole is after women. I just wish I knew what was going on with Gabe."

"Um, about that," I say. "Gabe was here earlier and told me what he was really doing in Montana." I wince. "It looks bad, Maddox, but I don't believe he's the killer."

"Fuck! Tell me."

I repeat everything Gabe told me, and Maddox frowns. "I can see why that would look bad. However, if he has a publisher lined up, they should be able to confirm what Gabe was doing." He pauses to put the vegetables in the oven. "Something doesn't add up. My brother hasn't told you—or us —everything."

"So, another woman has been found, and Olly is still missing, right? This guy is out of control, and that scares me." My stomach flutters with nerves at the thought of a killer being so close, possibly with his eye on the next victim.

Maddox moves around to face me, wraps his arms around my shoulders, and pulls me into his body. "I'm not going to let anything happen to you," he whispers in my ear. His words soothe my racing heart.

"Just don't let anything happen to you, either. You mean everything to me." I press my face into his chest and sigh.

His phone starts buzzing on the countertop at that moment. He grabs the phone with a heavy sigh and frowns at the caller ID: Branson.

My heart sinks because I have a feeling it's bad news.

MADDOX HOLDS MY HAND AS WE STEP INSIDE THE LODGE. My eyes immediately find Judean, who is standing beside Colton. The man looks exhausted, his shoulders slumped in defeat. I notice how close my friend stands to him, as though offering silent support. I feel sympathy for him, knowing he was the one who identified the body. I've never seen a dead body before, and I don't want to.

I scan the rest of the group in the lobby and see Richard with his arm around his mother. He looks like he's about to cry. I want to hug him, but I'm not sure if he'd want that. Besides, it certainly won't help with me standing here with the man I've fallen head over heels for. I never believed in love at first sight. Yet, I can't imagine my life without Maddox by my side. I shake my head, realizing how inappropriate those thoughts are right now. They just lost a daughter and sister.

Samantha was the woman Hunter found in the forest. She was dressed in Olly's clothes, which means the killer has Olly too. Believe it or not, Colton recognized her hands because of their long, bright red nails. He admitted that she had her hands on his chest, which he removed, so he noticed just how long the nails were. She had been hateful toward Judean and me, but I didn't want her dead. The feds and Branson were treating this case differently from their serial killer case until evidence said otherwise. Samantha had been beaten to death with a baseball bat. The others had bled and frozen to death while barely alive before being left to be found.

I swallow hard and turn to face Maddox. He meets my gaze and lowers his head. His mouth brushes my ear as he whispers, "Are you okay?"

"Not really." I briefly wrap my arms around his waist and squeeze. "I'm heading over to Judean."

He hugs me back and kisses me on the mouth. "I'll be over as soon as I can."

"I know. Just be careful."

"I will."

I kiss his cheek, offer a slight smile, and make my way over to my friend. We hug when I reach her, and my eyes go to Colton. I grab his hand and give it a reassuring squeeze.

"I'm scared, Sofie." Judean's eyes are swimming with tears. I'm reminded that she's known Samantha for a long time. "I'm sorry about Samantha."

She huffs out a sigh. "She was awful to me. All the time. She didn't deserve what happened to her, though."

I notice Judean's eyes stray to Colton and wonder if something good will come out of something bad. "Have you eaten?" I ask him.

"I can't right now," he admits.

"Why don't you go rest?"

He hesitates, his eyes on my friend.

"Hey," I say, drawing his attention. "Judean and I will stay together. Maddox will keep an eye on us. We'll be fine while you shower and eat something. I promise."

"Are you trying to tell me I stink?" He raises an eyebrow.

"Well, now that you mention it." I offer a soft smile. "Seriously, Colton. You look tired. Take care of yourself."

His eyes bounce to Judean again, so I nudge my friend, who has been silently watching our exchange. Much to my surprise—and, judging by the look on his face, Colton's— Judean steps into his space, wraps her arms around his waist, and gives him a big hug. He swallows hard before returning her embrace. "I knew you liked me." He pulls her closer and sighs softly. "I'll go clean up, but only if you two come with me. You're not leaving my sight."

Judean gasps. "You want a threesome!" She tries to pull away, but he won't let her. His cheeks flush red while I glance around us. Yep, she wasn't quiet at all. Great! I meet Maddox's gaze from across the room. He's talking with his brother, Spencer.

"Babe, when I get you naked, it'll just be you and me. I don't share." He snickers. "Besides, Maddox will kill me if I try anything with Sofie."

"As if I'd leave your sexy brother. He's mine."

"I'm glad to hear that." Maddox wraps an arm around me, and I rest back against him for a moment.

I tilt my head up to look at him and ask, "What's happening?"

"Branson called. A couple of hunters called saying they heard a woman scream. They tried to follow the sound, but they couldn't find anything, so they called Branson. The search has moved." He runs his hands through his hair.

"You want to be out there with him, right? We'll be fine here. I don't want you to worry. Besides, Colton offered us a threesome, so we'll be occupied for five minutes."

"Hey, now," Colton stutters. "One night wouldn't be enough with this one." He slides his arm around Judean, who doesn't push him away.

Interesting.

Cupping my face in his large hands, Maddox rests his forehead against mine. "Dad is expecting Colton, you, and Judean at his cabin." He softly brushes his thumbs over my cheeks. "You'll get to meet my mom." He smiles. "She will love you both." After placing a lingering kiss on my forehead, he pulls back and stares at his youngest brother.

"Bro, I've got them. I swear I do." Colton huffs, irritated.

"This is all your fault!" Richard shouts, charging across the room.

Maddox steps in front of me, causing Richard to stop short.

It doesn't stop him. "You're to blame for this, Sofie Ryan," he snarls.

"That's enough!" Maddox says. "The only person to blame is the one who took her life."

Stepping out from behind Maddox, I warily eye Richard. "I'm so sorry about Samantha, Richard. Her death has nothing to do with me."

He huffs and puffs, and his eyes fill with tears. I feel myself becoming emotional and step forward to put my hand on his arm. "I trust the sheriff to find the person who did this. I know it won't bring her back, but it will give you answers. I'm really sorry."

Pulling himself together, he shakes off my hand. Maddox grips my shoulders and moves me away.

"You're not sorry," he hisses. "You didn't like her. You wanted her dead so you could come back to me without her interference."

My eyes pop wide open in shock. What the hell has
gotten into him? He's delusional. "I'm not going to lie to you.
I didn't like her. But I sure as heck didn't want her dead. It's
awful to accuse me of that." I pause. "Besides, if I loved you, I
never would have broken up with you."

I turn my back on him, intending to leave with Colton and
Judean. However, Richard has other plans and reaches out,
grabbing the back of my jacket. I spin around to face him, my
heart pounding in my chest. "What are you doing, Richard?" I
demand, feeling a mix of fear and anger bubbling inside me.
His grip tightens on my jacket. His eyes are filled with a
strange intensity that sends shivers down my spine.

In the blink of an eye, Maddox's fist shoots out and hits
Richard square in the face. Richard releases his hold on me as
he falls to the ground. Maddox catches me as I stumble. "Stay
the fuck away from her," he says. "I will protect my woman
with everything I am, so heed my warning. You touch her
again, and you'll be joining your sister."

Wincing, I grab Maddox's arm and drag him away.
Catherine and Bernie, another member of the bachelorette
party, help Richard.

"Nice right hook, bro!" Colton hits his brother on the
shoulder. "Bad timing, but great all the same." He takes my
hands and pulls me toward Judean. "Bro, I'm going to shower,
and then we'll hang out with Mom and Dad. Keep us
updated."

Maddox nods in my direction, and I feel his eyes on me
until we're out of sight.

As we step into the garden, Colton says, "You know, I could get down with having a threesome with you two!"

"In your dreams, Romeo," I chuckle, relieved that he has lightened the mood.

WITH COLTON IN THE SHOWER AND JUDEAN RELAXING ON the couch, the cabin is quiet and peaceful when I step onto the back deck. Colton has a view of the mountains and the ravine below. I walk to the end of the deck and sit down in a very comfortable chair. Inhaling the scent of the wilderness, I sigh softly, closing my eyes and feeling completely content and at peace.

I settle deeper into my chair and listen to the sounds of nature surrounding me, wishing something evil wasn't lurking in the shadows of the trees. As night begins to fall, I worry about Maddox being out there with such a predator. I know the killer is targeting women, but that doesn't mean he isn't dangerous to the men and women hunting him.

A thud comes from inside, making my heart race with fear. "I'm being silly," I think as I shake it off. Judean probably knocked something over. My eyes grow heavy, and I struggle to keep them open, even when I hear the door to the back deck slide open. "Juju," I smirk. "I could sleep here."

She doesn't answer.

A bad feeling rushes over me.

I snap my eyes open to see what she's doing and open my

mouth to scream. But nothing comes out as the huge man dressed in dark green from head to toe covers my mouth and nose with a rag. I struggle, kicking and clawing at him. He's too strong, easily overpowering me. I try not to breathe, but I need air. Tears run unchecked down my face as the world goes black around me.

Chapter Twenty-Five

Maddox

As dusk settles and the stars twinkle in the sky, the moon is on our side. The aurora borealis shimmers in the distance, casting an ethereal glow over the landscape. I have a sick feeling in my gut that all is not right. I can't pinpoint what it is, but it's distracting me when I need to concentrate. Someone is stomping through the forest, heading our way. They sound like an elephant, which means its Branson.

I quickly knock Landon's arm down, gun still clasped tightly in his hand. "It's the sheriff. I doubt the killer would announce his arrival."

Branson appears, looking damn sick and panicked. Of

course, this gets my heart racing because he never looks like that. I meet his gaze. He swallows hard. "Sofie's gone."

"What? What the fuck does that mean?" Fear grabs hold of me as I stare at my brother, hoping he's wrong.

"Colton got out of the shower and found Judean unconscious on the floor. He went looking for Sofie and found signs of a scuffle on the deck. He carried Judean to Dad's and called me."

"I'm going to rip that bastard in half," I snarl, turning to head back to the truck.

"Where are you going?" Branson falls into step.

"How long ago?"

He knows exactly what I'm asking. "He was in the shower for a maximum of ten minutes. Five to quickly search for Sofie and get Judean to Dad's. I'd say fifteen to twenty minutes, tops."

"We're in the wrong place. If the bastard was around the cabins recently, then we need to start tracking from there. He won't be able to move quickly if he's carrying Sofie." I clench my jaw.

I continue moving, with Branson trailing me and shouting orders to the others through the radio. "The feds are going to head to the fire road," he tells me.

The fire road is five miles back from the cabins and the nearest road that gives us access. I'm torn as to whether I should go there myself and cut this bastard off. My heart and head are pulling me in different directions. If I'm going to find Sofie—which I will—I need to get my head on straight.

It feels like hours have passed since I left, but only an hour has gone by. I sit in the cab, and Branson jumps in beside me. I take a minute to settle myself. "He's going to pay, brother. If that bothers you, then you need to get out of my truck," I tell him.

He shakes his head. "She's your woman. That makes her family. I'm with you, but I won't let you go to prison. She needs you with her. Now, drive without killing us."

We fly down the road while Branson talks to our brothers. They're all in the forest, looking for a trail to pick up. The exception is Colton, who refuses to leave Judean. Dad stayed behind for extra protection, and Mom is there as well. I don't blame them. I hate myself for not staying with Sofie. She'd still be safe if I'd stayed.

I bring the truck to a jarring stop in my driveway and jump out. Dad jogs over and hands Branson and me a rucksack each filled with medical supplies, water, and energy bars. "Go get her, son."

"Thanks, Dad."

Branson strides off in front, and I follow. I know what he's doing. He doesn't want me to kill the son of a bitch. If that bastard has hurt Sofie, Branson won't be able to hold me back. I take a deep breath and keep moving, trying to clear my head of the anger and fear currently filling it. Branson suddenly stops, and I crash into him.

"Fucking hell, Maddox! You're like a fucking rock." He shakes himself and glances to the west before heading in that direction. "Someone has been through here recently. See this tamarack tree? Its color is more vivid than most. I noticed it when I hiked a few days ago. Someone has deliberately bent the branches here. The blue-green needles from the damaged branches have fallen into a puddle on the ground."

"That's a great nature lesson, but can we move on?"

"I was explaining why I thought they'd gone this way."

"I don't need an explanation. I just need Sofie."

Branson sighs. "Let's go."

The longer it takes, the more I fear what we'll find. Other than some broken branches here and there, we haven't seen anything. I voice my concern, "What if the asshole came through this way to the cabins, and he left this trail to misguide us?"

"I already thought of that, and I think this is Sofie's trail."

"Well, whoever left it for us is leading us straight to a dead end," I hiss, rubbing my brow where a headache is brewing that I've been trying to ignore. I take off my backpack, dig out two painkillers, and swallow them with water. I want to nip the pain in the bud before it gets any worse. I need to function without puking.

Branson eyes me. "I'm fine." I wave him on once I put the backpack on. The sun has started to rise, making it easier to see. Soon, we won't need the flashlights.

We reach the end of the path and trees, and a rock face appears before us. Just like I said.

"Should we check in with the other groups?"

"They'd have contacted us if they had anything."

"Just do it," I snap, running a hand down my face. "I'm

sorry. I'm desperate here." My voice cracks. Branson reaches out, places a firm hand on my shoulder, and squeezes it reassuringly. "We'll figure this out together," he says in a steady, calm voice. I take a deep breath and nod, grateful that he's here with me.

Chapter Twenty-Six

Sofie

MY HEAD HURTS AND MY VISION IS BLURRY, BUT I CAN TELL that I've been dumped underground. The air is stale, and the floor beneath me is hard and unforgiving. It's so cold that I'm shivering. It could be the fear. I hope Maddox tracks me and finds the broken branches. Assuming he knows how, that is. Tears trickle out of the corners of my eyes as I think about the man who has my heart. He's going to go crazy trying to find me. I know that for sure. I sniffle into the sleeve of my sweater, wishing I had something warmer.

"Hello?"

I freeze at the sound of a tentative female voice. "Olivia?" I whisper.

"Yes."

Dizziness overwhelms me as I push myself upright and look around the small room. In a far corner, I see Olivia huddled into herself.

Focusing on her, I recognize the pink slacks and white blouse with pink flowers that she wears. She also looks older than a teenager, which is how I thought about her after listening to Maddox.

"He had another woman. Made us switch clothes. He let her go." Olivia crises softly. "Why her and not me?"

I wince. "At least you're still alive."

She blinks and stares at me in shock. "She's dead? How? He wasn't gone long and when he returned, he brought you in here."

I frown. "What do you mean?"

"He took me with them in a truck. He let her go alongside a road, and then drove off. He brought me back here. I suppose he could have gone back after her when I slept. But he was here when I woke up. He gave me breakfast and then left. He was only gone a short time before he returned with you."

If that is true, then the timeline is totally off because Samantha was found yesterday.

My head aches as I rub my brows.

Olivia tilts her head. "How do you know who I am?"

"Searchers have been out in the forest trying to find you."

"I'm surprised my father bothered reporting me missing," she says sarcastically. "Then again, he won't want to lose his slave."

I frown, wondering what she means. "Olivia, does your father abuse you?"

She softly cries and nods. "And the others."

"Your brothers?" I feel sick.

"Yes."

I drag myself across the ground because I don't have the strength to stand. When I'm within arm's reach of the woman, I take her hand. "When we get out of this, I want you to tell the sheriff everything, okay? He is a good man. His brothers are too. They will protect you."

"We're not getting out of this alive," she whispers. "He's crazy."

"Do you know who he is?"

She shakes her head in response.

"How many rooms are down here? We're underground, right?"

"I think so. I'm not sure. I'm blindfolded when he takes me outside." Olivia lifts her head and wipes her cheeks with the edge of her sleeve, leaving muddy streaks on her face. Considering the situation we're in, I figure that's not bad.

A loud noise comes from the other side of the door, and our eyes meet. "He's coming," she whispers, her hands starting to tremble. "Don't look at him."

Metal on metal hisses through the door. When I notice the door starting to open, I force my gaze to stay steady.

The man is as huge as I remember, wearing a hockey mask on top of a Spider-Man mask. My mouth goes dry as he steps into the room, scanning the area with his eyes. Olivia's grip tightens on my hand, and I can feel her fear radiating off her in waves. We both know our chances of escaping this madman are slim to none.

"Say bye-bye, girls."

Fear claws at my gut as he rushes me, grabs my hair, and covers my face with a rag once again. I try to fight it, but I can't. I need oxygen and try to gulp it down, but everything goes black.

WHEN I WAKE UP, I FEEL WARM AND FUZZY, AND I HAVE A terrible headache. My body aches and feels stiff, and I hear a beeping sound nearby. I force my eyes open, but they close again due to the bright light.

"Turn off the light," Maddox says.

How can that be?

I sense the light fading, and then I hear him again. "Open your eyes, Sofie. You're safe now. Garrett's turned the lights off. Come on, baby. Let me see those gorgeous eyes."

"Maddox?" I whisper.

"Open your eyes," he says softly.

I flutter my eyes open and see his face hovering close to mine. I burst into tears and reach for him. He pulls me close, and I feel dampness on my neck. "You're here? Wait! Where is here? Where am I?"

Maddox pulls back, swipes at his eyes, and rests his forehead against mine. "You're in the hospital in Anchorage. Hunter and the two feds found you in the middle of the fire road. They called it in and got you airlifted here. I've never been so grateful for anything in my life as I was when I got the call that you were safe."

"Olivia?" I ask, but I'm met with confusion. "Olivia was there with me. You don't have her, do you?"

"Only you." Maddox kisses me softly, then drops into the chair beside the bed and holds my hand. "You're not leaving my sight."

"It's all a bit fuzzy around the edges, but I tried to fight back. I didn't have the strength. Wherever he took me, that's where Olivia is. We have to find her."

"Her family is still looking for her. Branson and the feds are trying to follow leads, but they haven't found anything yet. They sent some of the clay from your sweater to the FBI lab to see if they could narrow down an area to search."

Olivia's words came back to me, tightening my hold on Maddox's hand. "Her family abuses her. When she's found, you need to make sure Branson doesn't let her father or brothers near her. Promise me."

"We'll talk to Branson, okay? I promise we'll keep her safe."

I settle back against the pillows, my eyes focused on

Maddox. I'm aware that we're not alone in the room, but I didn't think I'd see him again.

My eyes fill with tears and Maddox becomes blurry. He brushes my tears away with his thumbs, but more fall.

I tug him close. "I need you to hold me," I mumble.

"I'll give you both some privacy," Garrett says. He brushes a hand along my arm. "I'm glad you're okay, Sofie."

Maddox takes off his boots, climbs onto the bed, and takes me into his arms. "I've never been so scared," he admits.

"It was strange. I really thought he would kill me. Yet I'd only been awake for about ten minutes when he came back and knocked me out again. Why would he take me and then let me go so quickly? It seems like a lot of messing around for no reason."

Maddox kisses me on the forehead and stays silent, holding me close.

I feel safe in his arms.

Chapter Twenty-Seven

Maddox

THE MOMENT I CARRY SOFIE INTO MY CABIN, MOM AND Dad appear and start fussing over her. Seconds later, Judean rushes in with Colton on her tail.

"Oh my gosh, Sofie! It was Richard who killed Samantha. You had a lucky escape." Judean slaps a hand over her mouth. "Oh! I didn't mean to blurt that out."

"What?" Sofie glances around the room in shock and forces her gaze my way.

I wince. "I wanted you to be settled before I told you."

"He really did, Sofie," Judean says, taking her hand. "I shouldn't have blurted it out like that. I'm still in shock from when you were taken, and then finding out that Richard is a killer."

Sofie swallows hard and pats Judean's hand. "Forget about it, Juju."

Judean groans and gives Sofie a hug. "I'll let that one slide because I'm so happy you're home and safe."

I sit down beside Sofie and put my arm around her as she leans into me.

Mom perches on the sofa beside me and squeezes my hand. "I'm Louisa Hawke. Would you like a warm drink and something to eat?"

"Not right now but thank you." She sighs softly and adds, "It's really nice to meet you, Mrs. Hawke."

"Oh, now! Louisa or Mom works just fine." She winks and heads back into the kitchen.

"I think Mom is making us dinner," I say.

Sofie mumbles. "I'm really sleepy. Can we go to bed?"

"Sure, baby." She falls asleep before I can move.

With Colton's help, I manage to put Sofie to bed. I double-check the window locks that Dad and Spencer had recently installed. I leave the door ajar and force myself to head back to the others.

IN THE MAIN PART OF THE CABIN, I FIND NOT ONLY MOM, Dad, Colton, and Judean, but also my other brothers. Agent Sheridan is standing close by, which makes me wonder.

Gabriel is the only one missing. I run a hand through my hair, feeling tired and out of sorts. I quickly glance toward the bedroom, feeling the urge to stay with Sofie.

Mom wraps her arms around my waist and squeezes tight before letting go. "Come eat," she says. She takes my hand, silently gets Ryland to move from the countertop, and urges me into the chair. "Now," she pauses while passing me a plate of sausage and eggs. "I want to know what the hell is going on with my Gabriel. I don't want any bullshit. I want the truth."

Everyone looks at Branson, who narrows his eyes as Mom grabs his face between her small hands and whispers, "Spill the beans, and don't lie to your mother."

Adele Sheridan raises an amused brow at my brother's predicament, which lifts my mood considerably. I continue eating, but I keep one eye on my brother because watching Mom pull the truth out of one of us is so awesome. I'm sure it only works because we love and respect her. She's one hell of a mom. Stubborn, too. I hope she's here in Alaska to stay.

"Mom," Branson says, taking her hands and holding them in his. "I don't believe Gabe is involved in what's going on." He sighs. "He lied to me and the feds, and that doesn't look good. But believe me when I say that I won't let anything happen to Gabe. I'm on his side. The feds know that without my having to say anything. I promise."

"It wasn't Gabriel," Sofie says, moving into the room.

I jump to my feet and meet Sofie halfway.

"I'm okay." She pats my chest and brushes her lips over mine.

"You didn't sleep for long." I sweep her off her feet and sit her in the chair I had been sitting in.

Mom rushes into the kitchen and plates some food for Sofie, along with a glass of orange juice.

"Thank you."

"You're welcome." Pause. "About my son—"

Sofie smiles softly at Mom and glances at Branson. "It wasn't Gabriel. The man was slightly bigger than him. His voice was rougher, and his skin was whiter than Gabe's. As though he's never been in the sun—at least not for a long while. I don't think I've seen him before."

Adele clears her throat, steps toward my brother, and whispers in his ear. Branson's eyes pop wide open, then close momentarily. "Fuck!" he curses.

"Branson Elliott Hawke, you will not use that language in front of me!"

He winces, and I hide a snicker. The others do too.

"Sorry, Mom. Adele just pointed out that we have a size fifteen boot print. Gabriel wears a ten."

"I told you it wasn't Gabe who took me." Sofie slowly starts to eat, and I notice that Judean has moved in close to her. I'm glad she has a friend. I glance at Colton and see that his brooding gaze is on Judean. I don't know what his problem is, but it's getting tiring.

I sit down between Ryland and Garrett on the sofa, lean back, and stare at the ceiling. I need sleep. Then I need to find my brother. I have a few ideas of where he might be, but I'm keeping that to myself.

"Maddox," Branson says quietly, his eyes flickering over my shoulder. "Agent Kalluk messaged Adele. Richard will talk, but only after he's spoken to Sofie. He hasn't said a word since he was arrested. His father is sending an attorney from Anchorage, but they haven't arrived yet. I want to get as much as we can out of Richard before the attorney gets here."

Spencer shakes his head. "Sofie shouldn't have to face that bastard."

"I'll be right there with her." Branson turns to Hunter. "You'll stand directly outside for added protection."

Hunter nods.

"We need answers," he says to me. "If there were another way, I'd take it. You know I don't want to hurt your woman."

"I don't like the idea of her being anywhere near him." I rub my tense neck. "I'll be glad when all this is over."

Glancing over my shoulder, I see Sofie. As though she senses my gaze, she turns and meets my eyes. I slowly make my way to her and explain what Branson wants. She loses some color in her face but nods her head.

"I'm still having trouble believing he killed her. They were always close. They defended each other. It doesn't make sense." Sofie winces as she stands up. "In the eight months I've known him, he hasn't shown any signs of anger or violence." She pauses. "Although, he was angry when I gave him his ring back. I thought he might hit me."

I clench my jaw when I hear that and watch as Sofie glances toward Judean. "What about you? You've known him longer than I have."

Judean replies, "He's always been the good guy. Protective of Samantha." She winces. "Occasionally, I've found them a bit creepy when they're together. If they weren't related, I'd think they were a couple." She shrugs. "At least that was before Sofie came into the picture."

"Go find the answers and then find your brother, Branson," says Dad.

"Wait?" Sofie glances around the room, a frown appearing on her face. "Gabe is missing?" The question is directed at Branson, who nods.

"You need to find him. He hasn't done anything wrong."

"We'll find him," Garrett says. "Then I'm going to knock his head off for hiding out."

Sofie worries at her lip as she heads out the front door, not looking back at anyone. I frown, catching Judean's worried gaze, before rushing outside after her.

Once we're in my truck, I see Branson and Hunter getting into their cars and leaving.

I brush her tears away and press a kiss to her lips. "Let's get this over with, and then we're going to have a soak in the tub in absolute privacy."

"I'd really like that."

Chapter Twenty-Eight

Sofie

I'VE BEEN NERVOUS SINCE LEAVING MADDOX IN HIS brother's office. I have a feeling that if the feds weren't here, he would have been allowed back. It helps knowing that Branson is beside me.

My hands are trembling, so I shove them into my jacket pocket.

"Are you ready?"

"I don't think I'll ever be ready." I swallow hard. "Let's get this over with."

The door opens, and there is Richard. He looks rough

sitting behind the desk. Dark circles under his eyes betray his exhaustion. His wrists are handcuffed to the table.

My legs quiver as I sit down across from him. Branson takes the chair beside me.

"I want to talk to Sofie alone," Richard drawls.

"That's not happening," Branson states. "You asked to speak with Sofie. She is here. That's as far as I'm willing to go. Take it or leave it."

Richard reins in his temper before turning to me. His eyes rove over my face. He takes his time appraising me while I sit waiting. I don't want to be the first to speak.

After a few minutes, he sighs. "Thank you for coming to see me, Sofie. It pains me for you to see me in here."

"Did you really kill your sister?"

"You don't believe I did it, do you?" He sits back as best he can with his hands cuffed. "All this time, my dear sister has done everything to get you to walk away from me. And you did in the end. She was never happy. She always wanted to be with me."

My brows pull tight as I hear things I've noticed and only vaguely wondered about. "You loved her. I know you did. She was your sister! How could you?"

"Do you want to know why I lashed out at her?" He winces. "I didn't mean to kill her, though. I couldn't stop once I started."

I stay silent because I honestly have no idea what to say. The man sitting before me is someone I don't know.

"She knew I wanted you back, and she didn't like it. She wanted me all to herself. She threatened to tell you about us."

"What the fuck!" I gasp. "You and Samantha were together?"

"We were never together, Sofie. We fucked. For a very long time. I thought I could have a normal relationship with you. Of course, Samantha and I still had sex often. Jealousy is a bitch, and I killed her for it." He smirks, showing no sign of remorse. "I found her on the fire road after the bastard had let her go. She thought she was saved. Shows what thought did, huh?"

My stomach threatens to revolt. "How long?" I barely hear the question leave my lips, as shock ricochets around me.

"Oh, you want the juicy details." He laughs. "I'll humor you. I was eighteen. Sam had borrowed one of my sweatshirts. I went into her room to get it back. I had no idea that I would find my fifteen-year-old sister lying naked on her bed, fingering herself." He claps his hands, delighted at his audience.

"She tried to cover herself, but when I offered to help, she relaxed and let big brother take over." He licks his lips, and I feel like throwing up. "She was an impatient little whore the moment I got my hands on her." He laughs. "Oops, I mean once I got my dick inside her. She was delicious."

"Yet you beat her to death. Your lover!"

"Yes, but don't worry. My father will get me out of this. He has before."

My mouth drops open in shock. Branson takes my hand,

and I wrap my cold fingers around his, needing him to steady me. This whole thing is a nightmare that came out of left field.

"I can see I've shocked you, but you'll get over it. Once I'm free, we can get married as planned. There's no need to postpone the wedding."

"Over my dead fucking body!" Branson roared, pulling me up from the table.

"Sofie!" Richard begs, rattling his wrists. "Tell him! Tell him we're getting married."

"You're an evil, manipulative man. I didn't like Samantha, but she didn't deserve a brother like you, and she didn't deserve to die. I hope you rot in hell for your sins."

On that note, I leave the room, followed by Branson. In the hallway, he puts his arm around my shoulders, and I lean into him. "I never realized how unhinged Richard is," I admit. "What's wrong with me?"

"Sofie, there's nothing wrong with you." He pushes me away slightly but keeps me close. "He's a grown man. He showed you what he wanted you to see. Nothing more. Please tell me you know that."

"I do." I offer him a weak smile. "He's damn creepy. I wanted to hurl in there."

"Yeah, he made my stomach turn, too. I sure as hell wasn't expecting that kind of confession."

"His father won't be able to get him out, will he? That was bullshit, right?"

"Total bullshit. It does make me wonder what he meant when he said his father had gotten him out of trouble *before*."

"I caught that."

"So did we," says Agent Adele Sheridan, joining us. "We'll figure it out. I never leave a stone unturned."

I glance up and see Maddox striding toward me. I walk straight into his arms and hold on tight. "Take me home."

THE SHOCK OF WHAT RICHARD TOLD ME HAS WORN OFF, leaving a sour taste in my mouth. I'm baffled that I never caught a glimpse of who he really is. I'm really stunned. I'm determined to put it out of my mind. I roll to the side of the bed, put my feet on the floor, and sit for a minute.

Maddox had lain down with me in bed but had obviously left once I fell asleep. He was probably too agitated to nap. Honestly, I didn't think I'd fall asleep either. I did, though. According to my watch, I slept for three hours.

I run my fingers through my hair and pad softly into the bathroom to take care of business.

I catch sight of myself in the mirror and pause. I look sleepy and sexy. A thought tumbles around in my mind. I smile to myself as I strip out of my leggings, shirt, and underwear, and put on a robe. I'm not sure if we're alone in the cabin.

It's quiet as I move into the living space. Maddox is sitting in the leather recliner, facing away from me. I walk toward him and sit on the arm of the chair. His eyes light up when they land on me, and he wraps an arm around my waist. "How are you feeling?

"Furious at the Walker family. There's something wrong with all of them." I let out a puff of air. "Other than being worried about Gabriel and Olivia, though, I'm fine. The nap did me a world of good." I glance around and lean into whisper, "We're alone, hmm?"

A hand slips into my robe and fondles a breast. "Lock the door." His voice is rough as he tweaks a nipple, sending a shudder of pleasure through me.

"Don't move. I have plans." I smirk as I quickly move to the door and lock the others out. I close the blinds, then slowly turn to face him, feeling a rush of excitement.

He looks delicious sitting in the large chair with his legs spread and a mischievous glint in his eye. His dark gaze follows me as I move closer and unfasten the belt at my waist. "Will you undress?"

He chuckles. "Your wish is my command."

"I wasn't quite sure how to get you naked quickly," I admit, feeling my face flush with embarrassment.

My mouth goes dry as more of his toned flesh is revealed. He pauses with his hand on the zipper of his pants. "Do you want me to take it slow?" he drawls. I nearly melt into a puddle. I nod, unable to speak. He holds my gaze, but I look down and watch as he slowly peels his pants down his firm legs. I bite my lip in anticipation, feeling my heart race and desire pool between my legs. He kicks his pants away and sits back in the chair, the leather creaks under his weight.

He is gorgeous, and every part of me clenches tight as I watch him fist his long, thick, rock-hard penis sticking up from his lap.

Swallowing hard, I lick my lips and drop the robe. His hand pauses, and his heated gaze roves over me. His eyes flick up to meet mine as I step into his space. I brush my fingers against his cock, noticing the lust in his eyes grow hotter. I smile softly and lean over him. His gaze drops to my breasts. "Fuck, Sofie!" he groans. He arches his back and rubs the head of his cock on the underside of my breasts. His breathing becomes heavy and erratic as I crush my mouth against his.

Our moans of lust are lost in the heat of our kiss. Gasping for breath, I pull away and push his hand away from his penis. I drop to my knees, and in an instant, I have him in my mouth.

"I'm so fucking close," he groans. "The things you do to me."

Smirking to myself, I take him deep. His penis is large, and it doesn't quite fit, but I'm trying my best. With my mouth full, I run my tongue over as much of him as I can reach, feeling him quiver beneath me. The taste of him has me wet and aching to be filled by him. Maddox pulls me off with a growl. He stands, lifts me up, and flips me over the back of the sofa. He thrusts into me with such force that I cry out with pleasure.

"Fuck, Sofie. Are you okay?"

"Don't stop," I beg.

His hands squeeze my hips as he pounds into me relentlessly. There is no finesse. It's raw and so fucking good. Leaning over me, Maddox whispers, "You're mine now," in my ear as his hands slide up my stomach and grab my breasts. I moan in response, feeling completely consumed by him.

The moment he pinches my nipples, my pussy clamps down hard, and I fly into pure bliss. I convulse around his rigid cock, enjoying the sensation of coming with him inside me. He loses his momentum and, with one hard thrust, his penis jerks repeatedly, releasing a warm rush of cum deep inside me. I shudder at the intense feeling, and then warmth wraps around me. He carries me to the bedroom where we collapse into each other's arms, breathing heavily as we soak in the afterglow.

"Fuck," he curses under his breath. "I felt that in my fucking toes."

I snicker. "I felt that in my pussy. You're dripping out of me."

He smacks my ass. "Your pussy was made for my cock."

"If you say so."

"I do." Five minutes later, he asks, "What were we talking about before you seduced me?"

I grin widely. "I don't want to think about anything other than us for the next hour."

I snuggle closer, swing my leg over his, and rest my head on his chest. His fingers trail lightly up and down my spine. The sensation sends shivers down my back.

"I love you," I whisper. He stops moving. "I know it's soon, but I do." I lift my head to meet his gaze. "I love you."

He brushes my hair back and says, "I've been in love with you since our eyes met at the airport. I knew from that moment that you were mine."

"Sure, of yourself, huh?"

"I wasn't back then. I am now." He drops a kiss on the tip of my nose. "I think I can sleep now." As his breathing settles, he whispers, "I love you, Sofie."

Epilogue

My head feels like it's been hit with a hammer. I wince. That's because I was. I groan in pain and try to remember what happened. I'd been hiking in the forest, enjoying the fresh air and nature.

While I was lost in my thoughts, a woman's scream caught me off guard. My heart dropped to my feet before I got my wits about me and took off in the distressed woman's direction. Not that it helped any. Before I could locate her, a beast of a man appeared out of nowhere and swung a large hammer. That was it. Lights out.

I shiver uncontrollably from the cold. The ground smells

of clay, making my nose twitch. I can still hear her screams echoing in my ears. I swallow thickly. My mouth so dry. I struggle to open my eyes and see anything in the darkness.

Other than my head, I don't think I'm injured, but I won't know for sure until I stop shaking. I reach out a trembling hand.

"You're awake."

I start at the feminine voice, yet I struggle to move and locate her.

"Don't move," she says. "You're hurt." She kneels in front of me and gently touches my forehead. "He gave me a dressing for the back of your head. It's not bleeding now."

The young woman has the deepest blue eyes, and although her blonde hair hangs in disarray around her petite frame, I find her stunning.

What the hell am I thinking?

You're not dead yet—that's a good sign.

"Who are you?" I ask, trying to focus on her face through the haze of pain.

She gives me a sad smile before lying down beside me. She wraps around me protectively, and she gently rubs my back. Her breath tickles my cheek. Then, she whispers into my ear, "I'm your guardian angel. I'll watch over you."

My shivers slowly subside, and I mutter, "I'm Gabriel Hawke," before drifting to sleep.

THE END

Thank you for reading *Maddox* and thank you for your reviews! It's really appreciated.

Subscribe with your email to be alerted about new releases, sales, and events.
www.lexibuchanan.com

OTHER BOOKS BY AUTHOR

Hawke's Ridge

Maddox · Colton (2026)

Den Hollows

One of Six · Two of Six (2026)

Den of Filth (New MC Series 2025)

Reckless Wilder (2026)

Fifth Realm Series (Romantasy)

Quiver of Chaos · Wings & Arrows (2026)

Standalone Romantasy

Persephone Unchained

Tallulah James Mystery

Dead and a Murder or Two · Dead and the Wedding Crashers · Dead and a Deadly Deed · Dead and a Best Friend

Boston Bay Vikings

Camden · Bennett · Ethan · Sutton · Carter · Bryson · Ivan · Theo · Noah · Knox · Jericho · Roman

Boston Bay Vikings Minor League

Lake · Rhodes · Nikoli · Dario · Madden · Bradford

Single Titles

Butterflies and Darkness · Come Back to Me · Indecent Villain · Lawful · Love Stryker · Tears in the Rain · Whispers of Yesterday

Holiday Season

Holiday Kisses in the Snow · Jingle Bells

Romantic Suspense Series

Twenty Eight Days · The Next Victim (2025)

Blossom Creek

Christmas at Emelia's · A Rake in Blossom Creek · Heatwave in Blossom Creek · Secret Love in Blossom Creek · Mischief in Blossom Creek · Runaway Bride in Blossom Creek · Naughty & Nice in Blossom Creek

Bad Boy Rockers

My Brother's Girl · Past Sins · My Best Friend's Sister · Never Let Go · Saving Jace · Silent Night (Novella)

Kincaid Sisters

Meant to be Mine · You Were Always Mine · Will You be Mine

McKenzie Brothers

Playing with the Boss · A McKenzie Wedding (Novella) · Playing with Fire · Playing with Desire · Playing with Trouble · Playing with their Hearts · A McKenzie Christmas (Novella)

De La Fuente Family (McKenzie Spinoff)

Love in Montana · Love in Purgatory · Love in Bloom · Love in Country · Love in Flame · Love in Game · Love in Education

McKenzie Cousins

(McKenzie Spinoff)

Baby Makes Three · A Business Decision · Secret Kisses · Kissing Cousins · If Only · Princess & the Puck · A Bakers Delight · A Cowboy for Christmas · A Secret Affair · One Christmas · The Pregnant Professor · It Started with a Kiss

Novella's

Educate Me · One Dance · Pure

ABOUT THE AUTHOR

While Lexi is the author of the chick lit series, Tallulah James Mystery, and the sexy wild Alaska series, Hawke's Ridge, she also writes romantasy. This author has over seventy published novels. Based in Ireland, this British author has been writing since 2013.

Follow on social media:

Website: http://lexibuchanan.com
Email: authorlexibuchanan@gmail.com

facebook.com/lexibuchananauthor
x.com/AuthorLexi
instagram.com/authorlexib
bookbub.com/author/lexi-buchanan
amazon.com/Lexi-Buchanan/e/B009SPA94U